THE ◆ GOD ◆ ENGINES

THE
◈ G O D ◈
ENGINES

JOHN SCALZI

SUBTERRANEAN PRESS 2009

First Edition

ISBN
978-1-59606-299-3

Subterranean Press
PO Box 190106
Burton, MI 48519

www.subterraneanpress.com

To Doselle Young

And gratefully acknowledging the efforts of
Bill Schafer, Yanni Kuznia, Tim Holt, Gail Cross,
Vincent Chong, and Cherie Priest

I t was time to whip the god.

Captain Ean Tephe entered the god chamber, small lacquered, filigreed chest in hand. He found blood on the deck, an acolyte spurting one and lying shivering on the other, and the god prostrate in its iron circle, its chains shortened into the circle floor. The healer Omll muttered over the acolyte. The god giggled into the iron its mouth was mashed into and flicked its tongue over red lips. A priest stood over the god, just outside the circle. Two other acolytes stood against the wall of the chamber, terrified.

Tephe set the chest on a table filled with discipline instruments. He turned to the priest, Croj Andso. "Explain this," he said.

Andso bristled momentarily. His nominal rank was not less than the captain's. But this involved the

Righteous, and thus Tephe's position of authority in this case was higher than Andso's.

"The Defiled was refusing its orders, and so I had Drian here discipline it," the priest said. His eyes tracked to the long iron pike that lay just outside the god's circle. A spatterline of blood trailed from it to the acolyte Drian. "The Defiled trapped the pike as Drian thrust in and pulled him into the circle. It bit him and released him only after I had it ordered driven into the floor."

Tephe addressed the healer Omll without taking his eyes off the priest. "How is the acolyte?" he asked.

"The Defiled took a mouthful of flesh from him," Omll said. "Off the shoulder. The bone is ripped out and vessels ruptured, and he has lost a lot of blood. I am sealing the wound but the wound is needful. Healer Garder will have to supervise the healing from here. His skills in this area are advanced of mine."

"Why did he not come?" Tephe asked.

"There was not time," Andso said. "Healer Omll happened to be passing outside when the attack occurred. He entered the chamber when he heard the screaming."

Tephe nodded briefly. "Apologies, healer Omll."

The healer nodded in response. "With your permission I need to bring acolyte Drian to the healer's bay."

"You have it," Tephe said. "Priest, if you will have your other acolytes assist the healer." Andso gestured to the other acolytes, who did not need to be told a second time. They lifted Drian off the floor and carried him out of the chamber, quickly. The captain was alone with the priest and the god.

Tephe reached to the floor and picked up the pike, examined the head. "I want to know how this happened, priest," he said.

"I already explained what happened, Captain," Andso said, tightly.

"You explained *what* happened," Tephe said. "I said I wanted to know *how*." He hefted the pike. "Where did this pike come from?"

"It was in our stores," Andso said. "I had it brought out when the Defiled refused its orders."

Tephe touched the head of the pike. "Did you examine it before you had it used?" he said.

"There was no need," Andso said. "Our supplies are certified by the Bishopry. All our instruments of discipline are second-made iron, Captain. They have to be. You know that."

"You must have marvelous faith in the Bishopry," Tephe said, "if you do not believe you must examine your own inventory."

"And you do not?" Andso said, straightening. The captain was edging into blasphemy, and that, at least, was in the priest's ambit. "Do you doubt the Bishopry, Captain?"

The captain glanced at the priest but did not reply. He hefted the pike again and thrust it savagely into the prone body of the god, the cutting spike of the weapon driving toward the flesh of the god's back.

The pike shaft bent; sharpened spike dragged roughly across godskin, catching but not cutting. The god giggled again, wheezy. The priest's eyes widened.

Tephe pulled back the pike and threw it on the floor, outside the circle, between him and the priest. "I do not doubt the Bishopry, Priest Andso," he said. "I doubt other men. You know that fleet merchants and suppliers are more concerned with cash than their souls. And you should know that profits made passing third-made iron as second-made are the difference between a good month and a bad one."

From the floor, a whispering sing-song. "'Third-made binds, second-made wounds, first-made kills,'" said the god, and giggled again.

The priest stared at the pike, and then looked up at the captain. "I want to question the quartermaster," Ando said. "He procured these supplies. It was his responsibility to ensure the certification was genuine."

"Quartermaster Usse is dead," Tephe said, sharply. "Along with three of his staff and ten other of our crew, in our late engagement off Ament Cour. If he is to blame for this, then you may be assured Our Lord has called him to task for it. You need not concern yourself further with him. And whatever his sins, priest, it is you who chose to accept a forged bishopric certification on faith. Your acolyte may pay for it."

"If he does, he will be with Our Lord," Andso said.

"And gloriously so," said the captain. "But I imagine at his age, not gladly." He kicked at the pike, sending it skittering toward the priest. "Destroy that," he said. "Pray over the ashes. And then go through your remaining instruments. All of them. I expect a full accounting by fourth bell, forenoon tomorrow."

"Yes, captain," Andso said, after a minute.

"That is all," Tephe said.

Andso look surprised. "You do not want my assistance?" he asked.

"This is a task given to captains," Tephe said. "Not to priests."

"Very well, Captain," Andso said, stiffly. "I leave you to your task."

"Wait," Tephe said, and motioned at the god. "Loosen its chains."

"Captain?" Andso said.

"Loosen its chains," the captain repeated. "I want it able to sit."

"I advise against it, Captain," Andso said. "The Defiled must be made low."

"It will be low enough when I am done with it," Tephe said. "Now, priest."

Andso went to the controls which unspooled the chain, and then released the lock on the chain.

"It is still on the floor," Tephe said, after several seconds.

"So it is," said the priest. "But it is so by choice."

"Very well," said Tephe. "Go."

The priest left.

"You may rise," Tephe said, to the god.

"To sit is not to rise," said the god.

"Then you may sit," Tephe said.

"The iron is cool," said the god. "It likes us well."

"As you will," Tephe said, and walked back to the table. He retrieved the small chest and walked toward the god, stopping close to the edge of the iron circle. He set the chest on the floor at the edge, in the line of the god's sight.

"Do you know what is in here?" he said.

"Treasure," whispered the god, mockingly, into the floor.

"So it is," said Tephe, and bent down to open the chest, to reveal a whip, flecked with metal.

The god hissed, slowly, sadly.

"You have not seen this before, because you have not given me cause to use it before," Tephe said, taking the whip, gently. "And so I will explain it to you." He held out the handle. "The handle is bone, taken from a god My Lord killed with His own hands. I have heard that My Lord took the bone from this god while it still lived. But I do not know the truth of it."

"We know the truth of it," the god said.

"The leather is godskin," Tephe said, ignoring the god's reply. "The skin of the same god whose bone serves as the handle. This skin was taken while the god lived, that much is truth."

"We knew of it," the god said, still on the floor. "The god yours killed. We felt its pain. We marveled at how long your god suffered it to live, harvesting bones and skin remade, sustained by despairing followers who could not bear to see their god so, but could not bear a life without it. So terrible. With the coin of faith and cruelty your god purchased that pretty, pretty whip. You do not understand the cost of what it is you hold."

"The gods do many things their followers are not given to understand," Tephe said. "What I do understand is that the bones and skin of a god alone do not make this something you would fear. For your fear, there are these." Tephe pointed to the splinters of metal, woven and embedded into the whip.

"Yes," the god hissed again.

"Single made iron," Tephe said. "It is as described in our commentaries: 'Born in the heart of a star, as it died and strew itself into darkness. Never collected to melt in the dust of aborning planets. Never made a third time in the fire of a human forge.'"

He held it closer to the god, but still outside the circle. The god flinched from it. "Look at the iron," Tephe said. "Unfashioned in itself but set and secured into this whip. And it is as you said. Third made iron binds, second made iron wounds, single made iron kills."

Tephe set the whip back into its case. "I do not know why this is. Why single made iron can kill a god.

I know only that it can. I know the gods fear death more than do men. I can kill you with this, god."

The god raised its head. "You do not name us as the others," it said. "You do not call us 'Defiled.' We have heard this before. We would know why."

"You do me service," Tephe said.

"But you do not use our name," said the god.

"I am not a fool," Tephe said. To name a god was to give it power.

The god smiled. "You do not even think it," it said. It set its head back on the iron.

"What I think," Tephe said, "is that you should swear to me that you will follow your orders. That you will bring us to Triskell, where we are expected in the morning."

"Why should we do this thing," asked the god.

"Because you are commanded," Tephe said.

"No man commands us," the god said.

Tephe reached into his shirt and pulled out his Talent, the iron cypher held by a silver chain. He held it toward the god. "Do not play games," he said. "You know well what this Talent signifies. On this ship I bear the Talent of command. It means on this ship, my word is as My Lord's. God though you are, you are yet His slave. And as you are His slave in all things, on this ship so are you mine. I command you in the name of My Lord. And I command you bring us to Triskell." Tephe placed his Talent back into his shirt.

"What men have you on this ship?" asked the god.

"I have three hundred eighty souls at the moment," said Tephe. The *Righteous* had been brought from Bishop's Call six months earlier with four hundred twenty men aboard, but battles and illness had reduced their number.

"Three hundred eighty good men," said the god.

"Yes," said Tephe.

"Then bid you them step outside your precious ship and push," said the god. "I do not doubt you will be at Triskell in the morning."

Tephe took the whip from the case, stood, and lashed hard into the god, the slivers of iron tearing into its flesh. The god screamed and kicked as far as its chain would allow. Godblood seeped from the gash.

"A lash for that," said Tephe, and after a moment lashed the god a second time. "And a lash for the acolyte Drian." The captain coiled the whip with the godblood and flesh still flecked on it, knelt and set it back into the chest. "If the acolyte dies, you will answer for that as well."

The god tried to laugh and sobbed instead. "It burns."

"It burns, yes," agreed the captain. "And it will burn further. Wounds from single made iron will not heal without the grace of the faithful, as you know. Your wounds will rot and increase, as will your pain, until you die. Unless you swear to obey me."

"If we die, you are lost out here," said the god.

"If you die, our Gavril will send a distress call, and we will be soon enough gathered," Tephe said. "I will be called to account, but the truth of it will be plain enough. Our Lord does not long suffer those who will not obey." Tephe motioned to the chest with the whip. "This you should know well."

The god said nothing and lay on the ground, stuttering and suffering. Tephe stood, patient, and watched.

"Make it stop," it said, after long minutes.

"Obey me," Tephe said.

"We will bring you to Triskell, or wherever else you require," said the god. "Make it stop."

"Swear," Tephe said.

"We have said what we will do!" shouted the god, its form rippling as it did so, into something atavistic and unbeautiful, a reminder that when The Lord enslaved other gods, He took their forms along with their names. The ripple ceased and the god resumed its enslaved form.

Tephe knelt, opened the service knife he kept in his blouse pocket, jabbed it into the meat of his left palm, praying as he did so. He cupped his right hand underneath his left, collecting the blood that flowed out. When enough collected, he stepped into the iron circle and placed his hands on the god's wounds, coating them with his own blood, letting the grace in his blood begin its healing work. The god screamed again for a moment and then lay still. Tephe finished his work and then quickly stepped outside of the iron circle, mindful that the god's chains were slack.

"Now," he said, holding his palm to stop the bleeding. "Bring us to Triskell."

"We will do as we have said," said the god, breathing heavily. "But we must have rest. Triskell is far, and you have hurt us."

"You have until eighth bell of the Dogs," Tephe said. "Tell me you understand and obey."

"We do," said the god, and collapsed again onto the iron.

Tephe collected the chest and exited the chamber. Andso was waiting outside with his acolytes. "You are bleeding," he said.

"The god has agreed to carry out its orders," Tephe said, ignoring the observation. "See that it is prepared to do so by eighth bell of the Dogs. For now I am allowing it to rest."

"We must first discipline it for acolyte Drian," Andso said.

"No," Tephe said. "It has had enough discipline for the day. I need it rested more than you need to punish it further. Do I make myself clear."

"Yes, Captain," Andso said. Tephe walked off toward his quarters to stow his chest, and then to the bridge, where Neal Forn, his first mate, waited.

"Have we an engine?" Forn asked, when Tephe was close enough that his question would not be overheard.

"Until Triskell, at least," Tephe said, and turned to Stral Teby, his helm. "Triskell on the imager, Mr. Teby."

Teby prayed over the imager and a map of stars lifted up, floating in a cube of space. The *Righteous* symbolized at the far edge of the map, Triskell diagonally across the cube from it.

"Sixty light years," Forn said, looking through the imager. "A hard distance in any event. I have no wonder why the god took its pause."

"We have our orders, Neal," Tephe said. "As does the god." Tephe rubbed his left palm, which had begun to throb. "Stay at post," he said. "I will be back before evening mess." He exited toward sick bay, to see if healer Garder was far enough along with acolyte Drian to tend to his own, smaller wound.

TWO

The gods have become restless," the priest Croj Andso said, to the officers seated in the captain's mess, at the conclusion of the evening meal.

Captain Tephe frowned. Andso was already on his third portion of wine. His was from his own stores, not the watered wine a ship's captain, by custom, furnished for his own table. The priest's wine was unadulterated, as was increasingly his tongue. And this last comment, pronounced with an unseemly levity, was at odds with what the captain had seen the god do to the acolyte Drian.

Before the captain could comment, Neal Forn spoke. "You call them 'gods,' Priest Andso," he said. "It was my understanding you were given to calling them 'defiled.' And that indeed you cannot be parted from the term, even at great cost."

From the far end of the table, Andso narrowed his eyes at the first mate. Forn was seated at the right of the captain, who sat at the head of the table. Andso was by tradition seated at the foot, although Tephe knew well enough that Andso regarded himself at the head, and the captain at the foot. Between the military and religious heads of the *Righteous* were the off-duty officers of the ship, who over the course of time habitually seated themselves in a vague approximation of their loyalty to either pole of duty.

Tephe had long noted the unconscious seating arrangement but neither said nor did anything about it. They were all loyal to him in any event, and he was loyal to His Lord. He did wish His Lord had not chosen Andso as His priest, or at least, had not chosen him to be His priest on the *Righteous*.

"It is not a difficult thing, Parishioner Forn," the priest said, his address reminding the first mate, as the priest often did, of his subordinate status under Their Lord. "They are gods, they are also defiled. When one is in the presence of our particular defiled god, as I often am, it is meet and appropriate to remind the creature that it is, in fact, defiled, and a slave, and bound to obey my commands. And the commands of the captain," the priest added, noting perhaps the incremental arch of Forn's eyebrow. "Among the faithful, such as yourself and the others on this table, we may discuss them generally and dis-passionately, as a species. Just as one may discuss dogs generally, without describing them as 'unclean,' which they are."

"But a dog neither knows nor cares if you describe it as 'unclean,' Priest Andso," Forn said. "Nor do we bid a dog to bring the *Righteous* through space or hold the ship and its crew safe from harm."

"If you have a point, Parishioner Forn, I regret to say that it escapes me at the moment," Andso said, swirling his wine.

"My point, Priest Andso, is that this ship has a god for an engine," Forn said. "A god who is angry and spiteful, and who will with opportunity do any of us harm, as your acolyte so recently learned. I am a good and faithful servant to Our Lord, as all here know, and hold no task higher than to bend to His command. Yet I am practical. Practicality teaches me that if one wishes one's engine to run well, one does not throw sand into its workings. Or in this case give it additional cause to hate us."

Andso took a long drink to finish his wine, and then motioned to a standing acolyte to refill his cup. "It will hate us regardless, because that is all it knows, and all it would know. And as you are a good and faithful servant of Our Lord, Parishioner Forn, of which I have no doubt," Andso uttered the last of these words with a unmistakable curl of his lip, "then you also know from the commentaries that Our Lord requires us to not only adore and honor him in the fullest measure, but to chastise and pity those whom He has brought low. 'They are the defiled, without measure of redemption, and faithful declaim their rank.'" He raised his cup to his lips once more.

"I admire your scrupulous adherence to the commentaries, Priest Andso," Forn said. "I wonder if you have a similar fervor for the portion of the commentaries which read 'He that has drink for a pillar finds it falls when he does lean upon it.'"

Andso paused in the motion of a swallowing and in doing so choked himself, spraying a little of his wine onto the table. An acolyte rushed to the priest with a kerchief; Andso snatched it, daubed his lips and chin, and flung it back at his acolyte. He turned to the captain. "You offer your first mate much freedom, Captain Tephe."

"I would think you would be gratified that he is so learned in the commentaries, Priest Andso," Tephe said, and then raised his hand quickly as the priest's face began to mottle. "Nevertheless I agree that this line of conversation has gone as far as it is to go. I am better interested in your first statement, when you said that the gods are getting restless. Perhaps you might speak more on this."

Andso stared for a moment, considering his next action. Tephe watched him, impassively. He had learned that given enough time, the priest would do the minimally acceptable thing; it was only when he was rushed that his arrogance overtook him.

Finally Andso forced himself to relax. "Very well, captain. After our incident today with the Defiled"— Andso shot Forn a glance—"I used the Gavril to talk to several priests on other ships."

"You engaged the Gavril without my permission?" Tephe said, straightening. It would explain why Lieutenant Ysta was absent from the captain's table this evening. Gavrils were given the Talent to speak to each other no matter how distant, and thus one was stationed on each ship of the fleet. Nevertheless, every God-given Talent took its toll with use, and it was wearying for any man to reach across space and find another single mind. If Andso had used the Gavril to contact several ships in rapid succession, Ysta might need a day to recover.

Andso looked back at the captain, mildly. "It was ecclesiastical business, Captain," said the priest. "And as you know, for such matters I may use may own discretion when using ship resources."

"You might have informed me as a courtesy," Tephe said. "The *Righteous* is without its Gavril now."

"Parishioner Ysta was fine when I left him," Andso said. He had returned to drinking. Tephe chose not to say anything further but glanced over to Forn, who nodded and motioned over one of the servers. He would have someone visit Ysta. "And in any event I learned what I needed to know, which is that our 'engine,' as your first mate describes it, is not the only one which has been refusing orders of late. On three other ships, the gods have also resisted or have had to be disciplined. This has all been since Celebration of the Immanence."

"Four instances in ten days," Forn said, returning to the conversation. "That does seem an unusual amount."

"When you consider that in the entire year previous there were but three such rebellions, it is most unusual," Andso said.

"Is there cause?" Tephe said.

"Of course not," Andso said. "Aside from these Defiled testing their boundaries, as does any trapped predator. They would wish to assert to us that they are yet terrible creatures, instead of the slaves of a greater god. They howl to the stars, Captain." Andso punctuated the comment with a heavy swallow of wine, and then pointed at Forn, unsteadily. "And this is why we must be constant in our reminders to them of their status, Parishioner Forn. Words. They have power. To name a god is to give it power. To deny it such is to take it. Only a little but even so. To celebrate Our Lord in its presence weakens it, and when we call this thing Defiled we lower it and raise Our Lord, because He is the one who enslaved it. You know, Parishioner Forn, what keeps the Defiled bound in that circle."

"I assume it is the iron in its chains," Forn said.

"It is faith, Parishioner Forn!" Andso said, too loudly. "Iron is but a simple metal. What gives it its quality to hold and wound and kill is our own faith in Our Lord. This is why I am here. To tend to your faith, each of you. And if every officer on this ship were as you, Parishioner Forn, the Defiled would have long ago slipped its bonds." Andso waved at Captain Tephe. "And then not even our captain's precious Talent of command would avail him of…"

"Enough," Tephe said, suddenly and severely. "Priest, you are drunk. I suggest you retire."

"I was already weary, Captain," Andso said, and pushed back his chair. An acolyte unobtrusively positioned himself to take the priest's unsteady arm; Andso angrily waved him away and looked around the table. "I will tell you something, all of you," he said. "A priest has no Talent—no thing of Our Lord to hang on his chest, to give him a Power. Do you know why? Because a priest is of Our Lord! His own hand, His own arm, His own tongue. I have faith, my parishioners. I am faith in Our Lord embodied. Faith, gentlemen. Without it we are lost." Andso glared directly at Forn. "I will see you on the morrow, Parishioner Forn. We will discuss your faith."

"Yes, Priest," Forn said. Andso weaved out of the captain's mess, trailing acolytes and the muttering of the table.

Tephe leaned toward his first mate. "I believe that your faith is strong, Neal," he said, quietly.

"Amen, so it is, Captain," Forn said. "Strong enough to survive this priest."

"He was a better priest, once, or so I have heard tell," Tephe said.

"I imagine this was before he made provision to travel with his own stock of wine," Forn said.

"I believe he makes such provision because he is aware how much better he once was," Tephe said.

"So," Forn said, and then shook his head, lightly. "I do not doubt his faith any more than my own, Captain," he said. "And I know he is the presence of Our Lord on the *Righteous*. I do wish Our Lord had seen fit to be present in a worthier vessel. If the priest is right that it is our faith and not iron that truly binds the god, then we sorely need our faith."

Tephe looked at his first mate with the very lightest of reproach. "Our failure at Ament Cour should not decrease our faith, Neal," he said.

"Neither yours nor mine, Captain," Forn agreed. "But our defeat weighs heavily on the crew, as does this rebellion by our god." Forn leaned in closer to the Captain. "And more than that they hear rumors of other late defeats and failures in the fleet, and that Our Lord is newly set upon by other gods. Priest Andso's foolish comment here at this table that other gods were restless will also find their way to the crew. Captain, the crew is unused to failure and defeat. Their faith is now put to the test."

Tephe sat back and considered his second in command. "I understand now why you deflected the priest into a pointless conversation about terminology," he said, to Forn. "And I acknowledge to my regret it is I who brought him back to it. My apologies, Neal."

Forn smiled. "He would have come round to it again on his own behalf. I but delayed him a moment at best." He became serious again. "My point, Captain, is that if there were a time where faith were needed to grow, this is that moment. Priest Andso is the man to whom such task is given. That drunken, petty, stupid man. I fear for it."

THREE

The portal to the Rookery opened and it was Shalle Thew, form bare beneath embroidered robe, who opened it.

This gave Captain Tephe a start. "You do not often answer the Rookery door," he said, after a moment.

"Yes, well," Shalle said. "Lade is having a meal, Cien is resting, Issa is ministering, and Tasy received a special dispensation to go to the Healer's Bay to tend that poor boy the god chewed upon. There was no one else to answer the door. And so here I am."

"I would speak to you if you have a moment," Tephe said.

"You are the captain," Shalle said, lightly, and brushed back a wisp of hair. "I always have time for you. It's one of the benefits of the job. Both yours and mine. Now, come in, captain, and be welcome."

Shalle stood aside, head bowed slightly, lips curved in a small smile.

The captain entered the Rookery. Shalle closed the portal and secured it. "We'll go to my nest. I'll let Lade know we're not to be disturbed. Go on, captain. I'll be right behind you." Shalle gave the captain a smile and disappeared into the Rookery's small mess area.

Shalle's "nest" was no more than the same cramped quarters any senior officer or priest would merit, save that where an officer's quarters were Spartan, and a priest's monastic, a rook's quarters were soft-edged, warm and inviting. Shalle's nest was filled with the colors of russet, purple and weathered gold, and the scent of fragrant and mellow woods. Tephe breathed it in as he always did and relaxed in spite of himself.

There was something new on Shalle's small vanity shelf. Tephe picked it up and examined it. It was a figurine of an animal he didn't recognize.

"It's a rook," Shalle said, entering the nest and securing the door. "A real one."

"Is it," Tephe said.

"A representation of one, anyway," Shalle said, and came up the captain, putting a gentle hand on his shoulder, and reaching with the other to lightly hold the hand in which the figurine rested. "It was a gift from Bran Usse, who found it on Ines and thought I would like it."

"A kind gift," the captain said. "And not what I would have expected from Quartermaster Usse."

"How do you mean," Shalle said, running fingers lightly across the captain's own.

"The Quartermaster was a severe man," the captain said.

Shalle gave a small laugh. "Not with me, my captain."

"So he was a man of two faces," Tephe said.

"No," Shalle said, with a tone that was both patient and gently mocking. "He had just the one. But we are all different to different people, aren't we? I know you're not the same with me as you are to your crew. It doesn't mean you have two faces."

"You are the same," Tephe said. "With everyone."

This earned the captain a quick but unhurried kiss on the cheek. "I'm glad you think so. I work hard to make it seem that way," Shalle said, and then slipped fingers around to take the figurine from the captain's hand. "Usse said that the shopkeep who sold this to him told him that in ancient times rooks were thought to guide souls after death."

"What did you think of that?" Tephe asked.

"It made me sad," Shalle said, gazing at the figurine. "Especially after Bran died so badly. I thought of a rook just waiting for him, sitting there watching him go." Shalle shuddered and set down the figurine. "I prefer how we think of rooks today. Not guides of the souls of the dead, but comforters of souls of the living."

"Their souls?" Tephe said, and now it was his turn to have a lightly mocking tone. Shalle grinned at this and pushed the captain to the bed; the captain allowed himself to be pushed.

"Yes, my captain, their souls," Shalle said, pressing into the captain. "How is your soul at the moment?"

Tephe reached over and drew Shalle into a long and welcome kiss. "I do confess it is better than it was," he said, when he had parted from the kiss.

Shalle lingered, eyes closed, smile on lightly parted lips, then moved away. "But not as good as it could be."

"You can tell that from a kiss," Tephe said.

"I can tell that from you," Shalle said.

Tephe smiled at this. "That quality of knowing is why I am here," he said. "Your rooks tend to the crew."

"Yes," Shalle said.

"And you to the officers," Tephe said.

Shalle smiled. "I think you're well aware of what my job is, and who is under my care, my captain. I see all the officers, and would see Priest Andso, if he'd ever step inside the rookery, and he'd rather set himself on fire than do that."

"How is their faith?" Tephe asked.

Shalle looked at the captain quizzically for a moment, then changed expression. "Clever of you to ask me that question."

"It is not my intent to be clever," Tephe said.

"No," Shalle agreed. "I know why you're asking. The attack at Ament Cour. The number of battles the *Righteous* has engaged in this tour. This attack by the god. The stories of other gods resisting."

Tephe was surprised. "The rumors are out already?" he said.

"Not rumors," Shalle said. "The Priest Andso was not subtle about using Lieutenant Ysta. It's all over the *Righteous* by this point."

"Stupid man," Tephe muttered.

"That's blasphemy," Shalle said, lightly.

"I did not say 'stupid priest,'" Tephe said. "I said 'stupid man.'"

"That's the sort of cleverness you say you don't intend," Shalle said.

"Neal—Commander Forn—says that the faith of the men has diminished of late due to these events," Tephe said, returning to the subject. "Do you see it? Do the other rooks?"

"We haven't been looking for it," Shalle said. "The crew comes here to have their release and to have their moment of joy, but you know that is not all we do. We comfort in other ways. By hearing and listening and allowing them to be the things they can't be when they are on duty or with their crewmates."

"And?" Tephe said.

"Now that you've brought it to my attention, many of those I and my rooks have tended to this tour want something else besides release," Shalle said. "They want that too, of course. But they also want to talk. They want to be held or touched without arousal." A wave to the rook figurine. "They give us little things and trinkets."

"They're worried," Tephe said.

"More than worried, I think," Shalle said. "Ean, you and I have been on three tours of duty together, here and on the *Holy*, and before that the both of us had other tours. Doesn't this tour feel different to you?"

"We have been given defeats we have not had before," Tephe said. "This would naturally give rise to doubts."

"I don't know," Shalle said. "The crew may have doubts because they are dealing with defeat. But it may also be that because we have doubt, we have been defeated."

"I am not sure of that," Tephe said.

"Neither am I," Shalle said. "But I get the feeling that there is something deeper at work here, Ean. It's been present since the start of the tour but I haven't had words for it until now. I needed you to bring it directly into my attention."

"And this relates to the crew's faith, you think," Tephe said.

"It might," Shalle said. "The men know what they know. They feel what they feel. In their souls, in the places where Our Lord moves through them, they sense what Our Lord senses. Our Lord is being challenged now by other gods in a way He has not been for centuries. If we sense in ourselves what Our Lord senses, then maybe we're all sensing something new."

"What is that?" Tephe asked.

"Fear," said Shalle.

"Now, that *is* blasphemy," Tephe said, after a long moment.

Shalle smiled. "A rook lives to comfort the faithful, or so the commentaries say. If speaking these words give you comfort, then Our Lord might forgive me."

"Of all the things these particular words of yours bring me, comfort is not one of them," Tephe said.

Shalle rose from the chair and let the robe ties slip, exposing smooth skin beneath, and leaned again toward the captain. "I don't believe that," Shalle said. "You are a captain. And you are you. When something affects your crew, you don't rest until you know what it is. Until you understand what it is. And so I speak understanding to you. If the words don't comfort you, the knowing does. And that's good enough for me."

Shalle hovered over Tephe now, robe open, leaning, slender sliver chain holding an iron Talent, hovering between small and perfect nipples. Tephe longed to take one in his mouth, and did. Shalle groaned and placed a hand behind the captain's head, pressing him into the nipple, which he began lightly to bite.

Tephe had longed for Shalle since they first met on the *Holy*, where Tephe had served as first mate. He was drawn first by words, carried by Shalle's warm and quiet voice, which rejected the careful distance and protocol of the High Speech favored by the Bishopry Militant, the cant which a young Tephe had struggled so hard to master and could not bring himself to leave off. Words slid, informal and inviting, from Shalle's mouth to Tephe's ear. Shalle's other qualities made them apparent soon after; not the physical—another rook was assigned to the officers—but the apprehension and intelligence and practical knowledge of a ship and its crew. When Tephe was offered the command of the *Righteous*, he requested Shalle to lead its rookery.

And he made sure to assign Shalle to the officers.

Shalle had disrobed Tephe with a rook's typical efficiency, straddled him, and took hold of his penis and began to stroke it. Tephe was confronted again with the rook's Talent, dangling near his face. He took hold of it.

"I still do not know what your Talent is," Tephe said.

"I think you do," Shalle said, and with a quick motion slid Tephe into the place they both wanted him to be. Tephe drew his arms around Shalle's waist and stood, causing the rook to laugh out loud and clasp hands around his neck to avoid the chance of him slipping out. Tephe turned and pushed Shalle into the bed, thrusting as he did so.

"This seems familiar," Shalle said.

"Enough," Tephe said, and thrust again, hard. Shalle's hands moved from his neck to his hips, bidding him do it again. He did. Shalle moaned in delight.

After they were done, Tephe's attention returned to the rook figurine. He picked it up again.

"It's not that interesting," Shalle said, draped across his chest.

"Not in itself," Tephe agreed. "But for who it is from. I still have trouble imagining Quartermaster Usse offering you a bauble."

"I thought it was very sweet of him," Shalle said. "He was a very gentle man with me."

"Then all of that gentleness went to you," Tephe said.

"No," Shalle said. "He spoke of his children with gentleness. And of his wife, though she left him. He said he always expected it and didn't blame her. It's hard to be married to a man who will never leave his ship."

"He never did leave it," Tephe said. "Until the end. Until he left it in a shroud."

"Let's not talk about that," Shalle said. "I prefer to remember him as he was."

"As he was with you," Tephe said.

"As he was," Shalle said, firmly. "Don't discount that part of who he was just because you didn't know it. None of us are all of who we are to any one person."

"What are you hiding from me?" Tephe said.

Shalle smiled and lightly slapped his chest. "None of your business. Obviously." Tephe laughed.

There was a quiet knock on the door. Shalle groaned, got up, found the robe and answered the door while tying its stays. A voice Tephe recognized as Lade whispered something.

Shalle looked back at Tephe. "Lade says the Gavril is at the door of the rookery."

Tephe frowned. Ysta had been dead asleep when Forn had him checked on, and should have been for hours yet. The captain dressed quickly and went to the rookery door, where Lt. Ysta stood, a troubling shade of gray.

"Lieutenant," Tephe said.

"CAPTAIN TEPHE," said Ysta in a voice clearly not his own. "BY ORDER OF THE BISHOPRY MILITANT, THE *RIGHTEOUS* IS TO BE BROUGHT TO BISHOP'S CALL. MAKE ALL HASTE. YOU ARE EXPECTED PRESENTLY."

Ysta choked, vomited and collapsed. Shalle slipped out of the rookery to attend him.

"He's all right," Shalle said, after a minute. "He's just worn out. We should get him the healer's bay."

"No," Tephe said. "Once Andso finds out we are to be brought to Bishop's Call, he will want to use him again, even if he is laid out in a healer's crèche." He nodded toward the rookery. "Bring him into the rookery. Andso will not step foot in it. Ysta will sleep all he needs. When he is awake, send him to me."

With that Tephe went to the bridge, to halt preparations for Triskell and begin the preparations for Bishop's Call.

To begin preparations for going home.

FOUR

C aptain Tephe nodded to the guards. "Open the gate," he said. The guards gave the order and the heavy iron gate of the landing citadel creaked open, revealing the city beyond it, and the mile-long thoroughfare connecting the landing citadel and the godhold on its other end. In between were tenements whose inhabitants hung out of windows and stood on street corners, waiting.

Waiting for him to parade the god.

Neal Forn came up to Tephe, bearing two bags, and handed one to the captain. "Your coppers, captain." Tephe nodded, and took the bag. Inside were coins, which he would throw to the crowds lining the streets as he passed them. They would reach for the coins with one hand and throw trash and rotten things at the passing god with the other, shouting as they did so.

"I remember being on the other end of this," Forn said, and gestured to the west. "I was a child six streets from here. When these gates opened, wherever we were and whatever we were doing, we came running. The captains and their mates would toss their coins and we would fight for them, and then take what we had and buy bread. When we were older, we would buy drink."

"You remember this fondly," Tephe said.

Forn snorted. "No, captain, not fondly. A thrown copper was often the thing that decided for the day whether I ate new, warm bread or what I had scraped out of a barrel to throw at the god." He jerked his head out toward the tenements. "This is not a place to grow well as a child, captain. I do not think half those I grew with made it to an age to leave, and most of those who grew to that age never left. I do not doubt I will see some of my childhood fellows down this street today, shouting pieties and hoping for copper."

"Toss them a coin, then," Tephe said. "They will praise you when they drink tonight."

Forn shook his head, and then looked out to the street. "I throw to the children," he said. "They need the coins better. And one of them might yet leave. As I did." Then the first mate gave his captain a small, bitter smile and took some distance from him.

Tephe gave him his distance and instead looked back toward the god, secured in an ornate rolling cage whose iron bars were too thick to allow the god hope of escape, but wide enough to let through the trash flung at it. Surrounding the cage were a dozen of the godhold guard, dressed in livery of red, gold and black, holding pikes of second-made iron. The pikes were meant to be ceremonial but were nevertheless sharpened and balanced for attack and discipline. Gods were known to attempt escape on their brief journey to the godhold, or their few remaining worshippers to attempt to rescue their lords.

Where either the gods or their followers would go from there was another matter entirely. The inner city of Bishop's Call was sealed by The Lord Himself, a mosaic ring of first-made iron circling it. No enslaved god, weakened and stripped of its native power, could hope to pass. Nor would The Lord's followers approach the ring, although for another reason entirely. While even the smallest nugget of first-made iron could bring a man more copper than he might see in a year, stealing iron from the Sealing Ring condemned the thief to have his soul consumed. Death beyond death.

Tephe shuddered at the thought, and looked up to see the god, in its cage, staring directly at him.

Between Tephe and the god Priest Andso interposed himself. "Captain, we are ready," he said. The priest was dressed in fine robes of green and gold and

held a long prieststaff in his right hand. The priest, Tephe knew, would parade close enough to the cage of the god to imply it was he himself who caged and controlled it, but not so close that he would be struck by the trash thrown at it. "We are ready," the priest said. "And it is a glorious day to parade!"

Tephe glanced at Forn, who discreetly rolled his eyes. They both turned back to the street, whose edges now swarmed with crowds, jeering and readying their refuse to hurl at the god as it passed by. The guards at the gate nodded to the captain; the gate was now fully open.

Tephe took a deep breath, jammed a hand into his bag of coppers, and stepped forward toward the street, and toward the godhold.

"Are you well, Captain Tephe?" asked Bishop Major Chawk. Chawk and two other bishops sat at a long, curved table of dark soapwood, sheaves of documents in front of each. Tephe stood in front of the desk, in a meeting room in the sprawling Bishopry, which in itself was nearly as large as the city which putatively contained it. "You appear distracted," the Bishop said.

"My apologies, Eminence," Tephe said. "I was recalling the parade upon our arrival."

"Ah, yes," Chawk said. "Did you enjoy it, Captain?"

"It is always an honor to show to the faithful the power of Our Lord, to whom even the gods submit," Tephe said.

Chawk chuckled. "A very politic answer, Captain. But you do not need to be politic here."

"Yes, Eminence," Tephe said, and kept his true opinion about that statement to himself.

"We have read your report on the events surrounding your defeat at Ament Cour," said another of the bishops, whom Tephe recognized as Stei Ero, the Bishopry's Vicar of Archives, charged with intelligence gathering. "Also your late addition of the incident with the god. And it will come to you as no surprise that we have collected additional accounts of both incidents, both from your ship's priest and from other sources."

"You have a spy aboard the *Righteous*," Tephe said.

"Does this offend you, Captain?" Ero asked.

"No, Eminence," Tephe said. "I hide nothing from the Bishopry Militant, or the Bishopry in general. Your spy will not tell you anything I would not. Therefore he is no harm to me or to my ship."

"You are indeed an honest captain," murmured Ero, who patted his stack of documents. "If perhaps not always a wise one. We might have expected better from the captain of a ship of the line than your withdrawal at Ament Cour. What do you say to that, Captain Tephe."

Tephe held himself very still. "I would say to you that we were engaged by three ships of equal strength to the *Righteous*, and at close quarters, and with a god who had lately brought us to Ament Cour and who was not at full strength, either to deflect attack or to aide us in escape," he said. "Through the grace of Our Lord we were able to destroy one of those ships and disable a second, all the while drawing the ships away from the planet itself and giving the faithful there time to fortify themselves against attack, and to call for additional ships to defend them. We left Ament Cour space only when the *Righteous'* wounds were too grave to sustain another attack, and even then our god had strength only to bring us as far as the outer planet in Ament Cour's system. We hid in that planet's rings, running dark and cold, until both ship and god were recovered well enough to travel once more."

"You provide us with a rationalization for your failure," Ero said.

"I provide you with an accounting, Eminence," Tephe said. "I stand here for my choices and will suffer any judgment they provoke. I chose within my power the wisest course of action for my ship and for the people of Ament Cour. Perhaps another captain would have done other, and better. These were my choices."

"Well said," said Chawk. "And in all, well done. You defended your ship and the faithful as far as you were able, and better than most would have done. This is nevertheless of bitter comfort. Before more of our ships could drive off the one ship the *Righteous* had been unable to defeat, it destroyed three cities on Ament Cour. Hundreds of thousands of souls lost in all."

"They did not land troops?" Tephe said. "Nor raid the cities?"

"Such was not their goal," Chawk said.

"What was their goal?" asked Tephe.

"Genocide!"

The word blasted from the third bishop, whom Tephe did not recognize. He did recognize the apprehension both Chawk and Ero formed on their faces when the third bishop spoke. Whomever he was, he outranked them both, and significantly.

"Yes, genocide," continued the third bishop. "A systematic eradication of the faithful. Not to make it easier to steal *things*, or to barter hostages for money, or to loot and rape, but to destroy Our Lord by destroying that which sustains him!"

Tephe glanced toward Chawk, whom to him seemed the most sympathetic to him on the panel. "What sustains Our Lord, Bishop Major?" he asked.

"Faith sustains Him, Captain," Chawk said, reprovingly. "As you must know from the commentaries."

"'For I am nourished by the faithful, and draw upon their celebration,'" quoted Tephe. "I know my commentaries well, Bishop Major."

"Then it is perhaps that you do not understand them fully," Chawk said. "When Our Lord speaks of being nourished by the faithful, He is not speaking in metaphor. Our faith sustains and strengthens Him, and gives Him the power to extend His grace to us, and to defeat and enslave His enemies, which in its turn allows us to travel the stars and find the space we need to increase our numbers and allow Him to grow more powerful and protect us further."

"And so to destroy His faithful is to wound Him directly," Tephe said.

"Even so," Chawk said.

"This is not in the commentaries," Tephe said.

"Our Lord is not a fool," Ero said. "He does not reveal how He may be wounded."

"Neither has a genocide been part of the tactics those outside Our Lord's grace have used against Him or the faithful," Tephe said. "This is neither in the commentaries nor in the military histories."

The bishops were silent as Chawk and Ero looked toward the third bishop. He in turn moved his gaze to Tephe.

"Prostrate yourself," he said to the captain.

Tephe fell to the floor, unquestioning.

"You are charged with silence," proclaimed the third Bishop. "What is spoken to you here is not to be spoken again, on remit of your soul." From the floor Tephe quaked; he knew this bishop was warning him that his soul would be consumed. "I charge you again with silence; and charge you a third time. You may rise."

Tephe rose.

"You have not heard of genocidal tactics being used because they have not been used for thousands of years," Bishop Ero said. "You know from the commentaries that in the Time Before, thousands of gods contested for the souls of the faithful and that Our Lord prevailed. What is not spoken of are the tactics these gods used in their attempts to diminish Him."

"Genocide was used by some, then." Tephe said.

"By all, good captain," Ero said. "By every one. And yet Our Lord still prevailed, and in doing so enslaved hundreds of the gods who contested against Him, and diminished the others so greatly that His preeminence was uncontested. These gods exist now on the margins of His empire, with only enough faithful to nibble at His feast. The looting and hostage taking of which we earlier spoke."

Tephe nodded. His earlier tours were a list of defenses against just such minor attacks and parries, and the goal in these engagements was twofold: to protect the faithful under attack and to capture rather than kill the gods who powered the enemy ships, so that they might be enslaved and thus used to increase the number of His ships.

"Captain, what happened at Ament Cour was not the first of its kind," Ero said.

Tephe looked at the bishop, shocked. "Other genocides?"

"Ament Cour was the third in the last month," Chawk said. "Smar and Breese also were attacked. Their cities and the faithful within were put to flame and fire. Millions of the faithful taken from the grace of Our Lord. It would have been as this at Ament Cour, save for your actions."

"Many still died," Tephe said.

"Yes," Chawk said. "But many lived who would not have."

"This is the first I have heard of these atrocities," Tephe said.

"You are not the only faithful of late enjoined to silence," said the third bishop.

"There was only one Gavril on Smar and on Breese allowed to speak beyond his own planet, as is so on every world," Ero said. "All of their messages come through us, here. It is not difficult to keep a secret if we wish it so, and we have wished it."

"It is not yet time to concern the faithful with this matter," Chawk said. "We prefer at the moment to have them believe that these minor gods and their followers are yet looting and hostage taking."

"With deference, your Eminences, this deception is not a thing which will long endure," Tephe said. "These minor gods have gone from small incursions to wholesale slaughter of the faithful. This is not a change in survival tactics. This is a change in underlying intent. Something has changed to take them out of hiding and into bald and murderous assault."

"Clever captain," Ero said, after a moment.

"I am not clever, Eminence," Tephe said. "I can read a map when it is laid out in front of me."

"There is a new god," Chawk said. "We do not know from whence it came. It has come to the edge of Our Lord's dominion. Its strength is considerable. We believe its presence provokes these little gods to misbehavior."

"They ally with it," Tephe said.

"Gods do not *ally,*" growled the third bishop.

Tephe bowed his head, deeply. "With deference, bishop, if what I have heard here is correct, then these gods are acting in a manner that suggests coordination and an underlying strategy. It does suggest an alliance."

"There is no alliance," said the third bishop, leaning forward in his chair. "*He* would know if there were. He says there is not. He says the gods hate each other as ever they have."

Tephe realized with a growing coldness who the third bishop must be. "Yes, Eminence," he said. The third bishop reclined into his chair once more.

"Whatever the cause for these actions, Our Lord has been lately weakened," Chawk said, drawing the conversation to himself. "His primacy over His dominion is not threatened, yet neither would it be wise for Him to ignore the threat that exists at His doorstep."

"I will do all that is asked of me to aid My Lord," Tephe said. "Though it cost me my life."

Chawk smiled. "We hope it will not come to that." The bishop produced an image from his documents and motioned for the captain to take it. It was of a planet, the coordinates of which were unfamiliar to him.

"That is your destination, captain," Ero said.

Tephe scanned the image. "There is no name for this place."

"Names have power," Chawk said. "Names call attention. We choose not to call attention to this place."

"Yes, Eminence," Tephe said. "What shall I find there?"

"Faith," said the third bishop.

FIVE

I do not understand," Captain Tephe said.

"Captain, recall for me that which the commentaries compare our faith," said Bishop Chawk.

"'Our faith is as iron,'" Tephe said. It was one of the first phrases children learned in their schooling.

"As with so many things in the commentaries, this is neither a shallow nor metaphorical comparison," Chawk said. "It is direct and accurate. The quality of faith increases its power, and its ability to sustain Our Lord. Your faith, as an example, Captain. It is the weakest of all."

Tephe felt himself straighten involuntarily. "My faith is not in doubt, Bishop Major," he said.

Chawk waved this away. "I am not speaking of the depth or sincerity of your faith, good Captain Tephe," the bishop said. "Neither is in question.

But your faith is the faith of your fathers, and their fathers, and their fathers before them, reaching back, no doubt, to the Time Before, when men chose the gods they would follow. Is that not right?"

"We have the honor of being First Called," Tephe said. "My ancestor Ordor Tephe chose to follow Our Lord and was martyred for it."

"A faithful lineage, to be sure," Chawk said, and Tephe sensed a slight air of dismissal at his ancestor's martyrdom, which rankled him. "That which makes your lineage proud also diminishes the quality of your own faith. Your faith was earned by your fathers before you, Captain. You wear it as you would a family coat passed down from another age."

"My faith is my own, your Eminence," Tephe said. "Though my fathers made it, it is renewed in me."

"Exactly!" Chawk exclaimed, and clapped his hands together for punctuation. "Renewed. Remade. As iron is remade in the forge."

Tephe now understood. "My faith is as third-made iron," he said.

"Not only your faith, Captain," Bishop Ero said. "Also that of nearly all of Our Lord's faithful. The totality of his dominion has assured that. Third-made faith is faith assumed, as your faith was assumed from the moment you were born."

"If there is third-made faith, then there is second-made as well," Tephe said.

"Faith taken," said Ero. "From other gods, when Our Lord defeats them, and their followers become Our Lord's newly faithful."

"Why is it more powerful?" Asked Tephe.

"It is not for you to question," said the third bishop, to the captain, rasping his words. "It is only for you to know. Even that is dangerous."

Tephe bowed his head.

"The theological issues of the quality of faith are not important to your mission," Chawk said, somewhat more gently. "Need you know only this; that for the purposes of sustaining Our Lord, third-made faith is moonlight, and second-made is sunlight." Tephe nodded. "As Our Lord's dominion has increased the number of faithful, so has it decreased the numbers of those whose faith may be second-made. Those numbers that remain would not be useful to Our Lord in his struggle with this new god."

Tephe looked again at the image Chawk had provided him. "Then I do not understand why you would have the *Righteous* brought to this place," he said. "If the faith I find there would not sustain Our Lord."

"The faith you will find there, Captain, is not second-made," Ero said. "Nor third-made."

Tephe looked up. "First-made faith?"

"Faith where before there was none," intoned the third bishop. "Faith pure and new."

"Faith which outshines second-made as second-made outshines third-made," Chawk said.

"How is this possible?" Tephe said. "Such faith could not have been since the Time Before. The commentaries tell us that in the Time Before all men chose and fought for their gods. All men, your Eminence."

"There are the public commentaries, Captain," Ero said, "which are given to the faithful to sustain their faith. There are the ecclesiastical commentaries, which inform the priesthood. And then there are the bishopric commentaries, known to few, because few need to know. Until now, you have known only the public commentaries."

"In the bishopric commentaries," Chawk said, "we learn that in the Time Before, Our Lord discovered there were some men without the knowledge of gods. Knowing that the time would come when He would need the power of that first-made faith, He secreted them to this place, hiding it from the other gods, so He could call upon the strength of that newly-made faith when He did need it."

"But what of the men there, Eminence?" Tephe said. "What of their souls? Thousands of years without the knowledge of Our Lord."

Tephe caught the quick glance Chawk shot to the third bishop, to see if the last comment aroused his wrath. The third bishop remained quiet. "Our Lord has made provision for those souls," Chawk said, smoothly but quickly. "Again, Captain, you need not concern yourself with theological matters, only with operational ones."

"As you say, your Eminence," Tephe said.

"Our Lord must tend to the incursions of this lately arrived god. He must remain within His dominion, and not reveal until the final moment this world to other, jealous gods, who watch where and how He moves," Ero said. "Therefore, He bids you to bring your ship to this world. Locate its largest settlement and bring its people to Our Lord. They must willingly accept Him."

"Am I bringing priests?" asked Tephe.

"There is no time for that," Ero said.

Tephe turned to Chawk, who held up a hand. "In other times, we might do," he said. "But for now, we must seek quicker and quieter methods. Your own priest is sufficient for conversion. We will furnish the *Righteous* with a company of Bishop's Men to assist you in your task."

The Bishop's Men—warrior acolytes, bodyguards of the ruling bishops, and, some whispered, those who by their task chose who would lead the Bishopry. "As you will," Tephe said. "I do note that many have chosen death over conversion. My own ancestor did so."

"These are men who do not hold to a god," Chawk said. "When you show them Our Lord's power, they will seize upon it."

Ero placed a small box on the table, and pushed it in Tephe's direction. "And when they do, give one among them this, and have your priest do his rites."

Tephe set down the image he held, took the box and opened it. Inside lay a Talent on a whisper-thin chain. The sigil seemed familiar, but Tephe could not at the moment place it. "May I ask which Talent this is," he said.

"It is the Talent of Entrance," Ero said. "Through it Our Lord will come to you and to His new flock, and take of them what He is due."

"It is a Talent not given often or lightly," Chawk said. "Be sure you choose well among the new faithful whom to wear it. He must with genuine and glad heart wish to receive Our Lord."

"Perhaps Priest Andso should choose," Tephe said, looking back down at the Talent.

"It is a task given to you," Chawk said. "Your actions at Ament Cour speak to your judgment and faithfulness. This is a mighty task for Our Lord. You were not chosen capriciously, good captain. And for your service, you will be rewarded."

"Your Eminence?" Tephe said.

"Upon your return, you are to be elevated," Ero said. "You will leave the common military and become in yourself a Bishop Major. You will with us plan the strategies that will assist Our Lord in defeating this new god and ending its nuisance. We will restore order and newly subjugate the gods whom this new one has made restless."

Tephe had stopped listening. To be elevated would be to withdraw into the cloisters of the Bishopry forever. To lose his command and crew. To lose the *Righteous*.

To lose Shalle.

Tephe covered the Talent he had been given and placed its box back on the table. "You do me too much honor," he said. "I could not ask to be elevated for the simple task of performing my duties as they should be performed."

"What you would *ask* is of no consequence here," said the third bishop.

"Captain Tephe, already much has been revealed to you that is not given to one such as yourself to know," Ero said. "Only the extraordinary nature of the mission compels this breach. You are allowed to know this knowledge only because it has been decided that you are to become as we are."

"And glad you should be for it," Chawk said. "As we are. Rare is it in these times for a Bishop Major to come from the ranks of the common military. You will bring to our strategies a perspective fresh and well-needed. This will be a benefit to us as much as an elevation of yourself."

Tephe closed his eyes and ducked his head and prayed that the bishops looking on him would see humility and not anguish in his action. After a moment, he looked up again.

"'Every thing we do is for the glory of Our Lord,'" he quoted.

It was only after he found himself on the cobble-stones, ears ringing, that Tephe was aware a bomb had gone off.

Tephe quickly checked his body and found he was not injured. He rolled off his back in time to see to a woman lunging toward him, knife in hand. Her scream was muted by the injury to his ears. Tephe kicked out with full force and brought the sole of his boot into her knee. The knee twisted in an unnatural direction and the woman fell, knife clattering from her hand. Tephe scrambled up as another woman, seeing the first woman fall, changed course toward the captain, howling.

Tephe waited until the woman was close enough, and then grabbed the bag of coppers on the road, given to him to throw from during the parade back to the landing citadel. Tephe swung, and the bag connected hard into the woman's temple, knocking her off balance even as it tore open, showering coins into the air and street. The woman staggered at the blow, and Tephe used the opening to push her down into the street. The woman's head connected with the cob-blestones with the sound of a melon fruit falling from a table. She stopped moving. Tephe found the knife the first woman had dropped, grabbed it and held it ready as he observed the scene.

Near himself, Tephe saw Neal Forn sitting in the street, clutching a bleeding wound on his head; Forn saw his captain looking at him and signaled he was not seriously injured. Tephe turned his attention back down the street.

The bomb had gone off well behind the captain and toward the cage which held the god. On the street lay an acolyte and two godhold guards, one torn near in half. Either the bomb had been a small one or he had fallen on it to protect others. Behind that carnage the remaining guard engaged a band of ragged street fighters, wielding knives and common, blunt tools. They surrounded the caged god, who was itself looking about, as if in a panic.

What is it looking for? thought Tephe.

The god grinned madly and rushed to the front left side of its enclosure, and extended an arm through its cage bars, as if reaching for something.

Tephe followed the god's gaze back into the street, where a hooded figure had stepped out of the chaos of bystanders running from the bomb. The figure held something tightly in its hand. Tephe looked back to the god and saw it motioning to figure, bidding it to throw what it had.

The figure was looking toward the god, away from Tephe. The captain ran toward the figure as quickly as he could, knife in hand, as the figure cocked back its arm and readied for the throw.

Tephe connected with the figure just before the top of its throw, the object, its arc aborted, skittering onto the cobblestones a few yards in front of them. The figure lost its balance but did not fall, the hood of its cape falling back to reveal a middle-aged woman with scars on her face. The woman righted herself quickly and equally quickly put a fist into the captain's mouth, causing him to fall back, howling and clutching his mouth, dropping the knife as he did so. The woman frantically scanned the street, looking for the fallen object she had held in her hand.

Tephe, feeling the blood on his lips, followed her gaze and lunged when she did, aiming for her, not whatever she was looking for. He pushed his mass into hers as they both dove, the captain's larger body winning the physical argument. The woman collided into the cobblestones, with a great cough of air forcing itself out of her body. Tephe rolled away from her to prepare himself for an attack. As he did so he felt something jab itself uncomfortably into in his back. Tephe arched, slid a hand underneath himself, grabbed at the object and held onto it as he rolled again, facing down.

As he did he felt a sharp weight land on his spine, almost breaking it. The air vomited out of his lungs. Tephe was in too much pain to move. Hands reached to the back of his head, jerking it up and slamming his face into the cobblestones. Tephe felt his nose give way and the skin on his forehead abrade. The woman pulled his head back a second time. She would pound his head into the street until he was dead.

There was a gasp above Tephe, and then a splash of wet warmth on the back of his neck. Tephe turned his head painfully to see the woman collapse onto the street next to him, blood falling out of a heavy cut across her neck. He rolled away from her, facing up, and saw Neal Forn above him, wielding the knife the captain had taken from the woman who had first attacked him.

"It was a woman," Forn said, breathing heavily from exertion. "They were all women, captain."

Tephe nodded, propped himself up, turned to the side and retched. "Women could get closer to the parade," he said. "The guards would not have expected them to attack. Or to fight." He groggily looked toward the god's cage. The women who had been fighting there had dispersed, save for the ones who were in the street, dead.

"It makes no sense," Forn said. "A circle of first-made iron surrounds this whole area. There would have nowhere for the god to go. There was no escape to be had."

Tephe felt the object in his hand, and opened his hand to see it. It was a Talent on a chain.

"Perhaps escape was not what it wanted," he said.

SIX

Y ou may have fooled the godhold's Captain of the Guards, but I am not so easily fooled," Priest Andso said to Captain Tephe. The two stood at the door of the god's chamber on the *Righteous*. "And if you will question the god, then I will be there as well."

Tephe, still in pain from the healer's ministering of his wounds, kept his temper in check but was inwardly irritated with himself. He had indeed withheld from the godhold captain, choosing to keep secret the Talent he had taken from the woman. It was a key to a larger plan, one he would not discover if he were to give it up. A plan that involved the god of the *Righteous*, and therefore the *Righteous* itself.

"I saw it, Captain," said Andso. "That thing which you took from the woman. During the battle. I saw it. I know it well involves the god."

"Strange how much you saw of the battle from your vantage point under a cart," Tephe said, naming the place the priest had been discovered in the aftermath.

Andso flared. "Do not blaspheme, Captain Andso."

"It is not blasphemy to speak the truth, priest," Tephe said. He started to push past Andso.

Andso blocked him. "Indeed, Captain," said the priest. "Here is a truth for you, then. You are captain and commander of this ship. But by the rights of the priesthood and the rules of the Bishopry Militant, you must have the blessings and prayers of a priest before your ship can leave port. You must have my blessing, Captain, or the *Righteous* will not move an inch."

"This ship's orders come directly from the Speaker," Tephe said, finally naming to himself the third bishop, the sole bishop who spoke directly to The Lord and who therefore carried His word and His orders, uncontested. Tephe watched the priest's eyes widen involuntarily. "You need to ask yourself, Priest Andso, whether you wish to be the one to explain to him why this ship has not budged when he has bid it depart."

The priest looked panicked for a moment. Then he smiled at the captain. "By all means, Captain

Tephe, let us raise the Bishopry Militant," he said. "I will explain why I have delayed our departure. And you may explain why you lied to the Captain of the Guards and even now hold a trinket meant for the god. Perhaps you intend to deliver it after all."

It was Tephe's turn to flare. "Call me a traitor again, priest," he said, moving his face directly into the other man's own. "You will know my response, and gladly will I answer to Our Lord Himself for it."

Andso swallowed but held his ground. "This ship will not move, captain, until I know what business you have with the god."

Tephe swore and withdrew momentarily, and then stormed back up to the priest. Then he paused and thought better of what he was about to say.

The priest smiled. "We have understanding, then," he said, to Tephe.

Tephe said nothing but opened the portal to the god's chamber and bid the priest enter.

Inside was the god, chained and resting in its circle, and two acolytes standing guard with pikes. Captain Tephe wondered briefly if the pikes were finally genuine second-made iron. "Get out," he said to the acolytes. The two looked to their priest, who nodded. The two carefully set down their pikes outside the god's iron circle and departed, closing the portal behind them.

Tephe knelt, drew an object from his blouse pocket and showed it to the god.

"What is this," he asked.

The god turned its head idly and glanced at the thing, briefly. "A pretty thing," it said, looking away again. "A trinket. A thing of no importance."

Tephe held the object closer to the god, edging the iron circle itself. "This is a Talent," he said. "A thing gods give followers to channel their grace, so the followers may use that grace to their own ends."

"Perhaps," the god said.

"This is a Talent you gave to your own followers," Tephe said.

"Perhaps," the god rather extravagantly yawned and made to lay in its circle, as if to sleep.

"Talents hold no power in themselves," Tephe said. "If a god does not choose to allow it, its grace does not flow to one. If a god is enslaved, all its Talents sleep forever."

"A master you are of things which hold no interest to us," the god said. "A master of rules. Of little bindings. Of trivium. Of useless things."

"Indeed," said the captain. "This is a thing of no use. Certainly not to the god who created it. And yet if this thing is of so little importance, then it is passing strange a dozen women died attempting to bring it to you."

From the floor the god shrugged. "We cannot say why women do as they do," it said. "Nor men. You are all without sense to us. We do not see why *your lord*"—the words, spit as venom—"holds you so dear. Boring little creatures, you are."

"You will answer me," Tephe said. "You will tell me what this thing is to you."

"We have already answered and told," the god said. "Ask us again, and we will answer these words to you once more. If we do not fall asleep."

Tephe stared at the god grimly for a moment and turned slightly toward the other man in the room. "Tell me, priest"—he began, and in turning, let the Talent he lightly held graze into the air above the iron circle.

The god snarled something high-pitched and shattering and snatched viciously at the Talent; only the fact the captain had held it so lightly kept him from losing his hand at the wrist. The Talent was airborne for the briefest of moments, the arc of its path exceeding the height of the god's chains. It fell, and the god lunged at it, grabbing at it with one hand and then pulling it toward itself, clasping it to its bosom. The god wheeled its head around to glare ferally at the captain, a triumphant grin pulling back its lips to reveal teeth.

Then the god screamed, hideously, and flung the Talent from itself. It clattered across the floor as it exited the iron circle. The god fell to the ground, tearing itself at the places the Talent touched.

Captain Tephe watched all of this, calmly. He glanced toward the priest, who was both terrified and fascinated, torn between fleeing the room, and watching the god tear into itself, leaving gobbets of its godflesh on the iron of its circle.

After a minute of this, Tephe went to the table which controlled the length of the god's chains, and contracted them all to the floor. The god lay, spread out, writhing as it rubbed the places the Talent touched, hard on the iron. Tephe left the table, retrieved the Talent, and knelt, showing it to the twisting god once more.

"This Talent is my own," he said. "Given to me by My Lord when I was placed as master of this ship. In your studied disinterest and in your haste to claim it, you did not recognize it for what it was. Because it is of My Lord, it burned you when you held it to you, as you would be burned by a Talent of any other god."

Tephe reached around his neck and removed a second Talent, and showed it to the god. The god cried and bucked in its chains, trying to gain purchase against its restraints to raise itself. It failed, slipping against its own godblood. Tephe held the Talent well outside the iron circle in any event.

"This is the Talent you seek," Tephe said. "I would know why you want it."

"It is ours!" screamed the god.

"It is yours but it is of no use to you," Tephe said. "To whom would you give it? And to what end? Your grace is gone. You could not help your followers even if you wished it. Why must you have this Talent?"

The god howled and writhed and spit but would not answer. Tephe put the god's Talent into his blouse and his own back around his neck.

In time the god quieted down. "We are hurt," it said. "You have hurt us again. Heal us."

"No," said Tephe. "These wounds you keep until you heal them yourself. Remember them. Remember also that your tricks and schemes will not avail you here. You are set to our service and you will give it." He rose. "We will leave here before the end of the watch. Heal yourself and be ready for the direction I give you then."

"What of our Talent?" said the god.

"It is no longer yours," Tephe said. "I should have it presented to My Lord when it came to me. I regret not having done. I will have it destroyed instead."

From the iron, the god wept. Tephe turned and left the god's chamber, Priest Andso trailing behind.

The priest turned to the captain as the latter sealed the chamber portal. "You did not mean what you said to the Defiled," he said. "About destroying the Talent."

"I meant it in earnest," Tephe said. "By your insistence, priest, you were in that chamber. You saw how it grasped for the Talent when I gave it the slimmest of chances. You saw the triumph in its eyes when it thought it had gained it for its own. And so long as it exists, followers of this god will hunt for it, that much is clear. Whatever this Talent is, it is a danger to us and the *Righteous* so long as it is on this ship. Destroying it is the only course."

"You would destroy it now, yet you risked your own command to keep it secret," Andso said.

"That is because I thought I could get knowledge from the god about it," Tephe said.

"That knowledge is still lacking," Andso said.

"No, priest," Tephe said. "I did not go into that chamber expecting the creature to speak the truth of it to me. Its actions were what would speak, and did. The attack on the street could have been nothing more than the fervor of believers mortgaging their lives to free their god." Tephe fished out the Talent from his blouse and showed it to the priest. "The god's desire for this says it was not. It plans for something to happen, some event for which it is to play a part, and to which this is a key."

"We do not know how," said Andso.

"We do not need to know how," Tephe said. "If the creature lacks the key, the event cannot happen. It needs this"—Tephe motioned with the Talent—"and we have means to deprive it what it needs, and in doing so destroy the event and the threat to this ship. I will do so." He turned to go.

Andso reached for the captain's elbow. "Let us destroy this key," he said. "But first let me examine it. You spoke truly, captain, when you said this thing has no power in itself. No grace can flow to it. Yet it has power in some fashion, else the Defiled would not desire it so. If we could learn what that power is, it would be intelligence of benefit to Our Lord, and to the Bishopry Militant."

"It would be intelligence of benefit to you as well, I expect, Priest Andso," Tephe said.

The priest straightened himself. "Not all are so marked for easy advancement as you, Captain," he said. "If our coming task indeed comes from the Speaker himself, there is no doubt that if it is successful you will reap the benefit and will leave command of this ship behind you."

"If it is to be so," Tephe said. "I am content to be the captain of the *Righteous* for a good while longer."

"Indeed," Andso said, and could not keep the lightest of sneers out of his voice. "There are others of us who would hope for a rather quicker path from her holds, and if I may be so bold, nor do I believe that some of us would be greatly missed. If all of this is accomplished while yet you remain in command, then how much better that all of Our Lord's faithful on the *Righteous* might receive what they would wish: you remaining and me going."

Tephe glanced at the Talent, considering.

"A few days, captain," Andso said. "And in that time, not an argument or objection or raised eyebrow. A little time is all I ask, to make my fortune as your fortune is already made. In doing so, your fortunes can only rise. Perhaps they will rise so far they will let you keep the *Righteous* after all." He placed his hand out to receive the Talent.

Tephe gave it to the priest. "A few days," he said. "When I say it is to be destroyed, it will be. That is not a matter of debate."

"No," Andso said, gazing at the Talent. "No debate. A little time is all I need."

"Keep it well away from the god," Tephe said.

"Of course, Captain," Andso said. "Thank you. My blessing upon you." He walked away, toward the priest quarters.

Tephe headed to the bridge and at the last moment turned toward the Rookery. When he arrived he pounded upon the portal rather than keying the chime. Issa answered, saw the look on the captain's face, and called for Shalle.

Shalle came to the door, face open and curious. Tephe brought his lips down before Shalle could utter words, pressing them both against the portal. Issa stood to the side, eyes wide; if anyone other than the captain were to engage a rook outside a nest, a lash of punishment would be the least of his problems.

"It's nice to see you too," Shalle said, when the captain broke his kiss.

"I need to be with you," Tephe said.

Shalle listened, as much to the quality of his voice as the words he spoke, said, "Yes, I think you do," and gently pulled the captain inside the rookery. Issa closed the portal behind them.

CHAPTER

SEVEN

Y ou have command," Captain Tephe said abruptly, to Neal Forn. He stood from his chair.

"Sir," Forn said, impassively, but fixed his captain with the slightest of inquiring eyebrows. The *Righteous* was moments away from being brought to the unnamed planet. Forn had commanded at such times before, but always on his own watch. In any event it was not a convenient time for a captain to quit his station.

Tephe chose not to respond to his first mate's unspoken inquiry. Forn would have to get used to doing things without him; if Tephe had any say in it, Forn would soon be captain of the *Righteous*. More than that, Tephe simply did not have an interest in explaining himself at the moment. He left the bridge without saying another word.

In the corridors of the *Righteous* were the hum and clatter of industry, as its crew—*his* crew, for what little time remained to him, Tephe thought—made its preparations for transport and landing. The crew had been informed that the *Righteous* had been chosen for a mission at the direct order of the Speaker, and the news had lifted their spirits and had grown their faith; the chatter and movement of the crew had regained the confidence that had been sapped by Ament Cour and by hard months onboard. Tephe warmed his own cold doubts in the new sureness of their work, nodding to the crew as they acknowledged his presence among them.

Tephe stopped at the portal of the god's chamber, and heard a low murmur inside.

He entered.

If Priest Andso was surprised to see the captain of the *Righteous* in the god chamber, he gave no indication. Andso's acolytes were not so impassive, but neither of them took more than a small pause in their recitations to note Tephe's arrival before returning to their task. The voices of the priest and acolytes rose and fell, called and responded, praying to the glory of Their Lord, and using His power to compel the *Righteous'* captive god to bring them to where they wished to go.

Tephe turned his attention from the priest and the acolytes and to the god, who stood, simply, motionless, quiet, its eyes closed. Tephe did not pretend to understand how the god did what it did to bring them from one point in space to another, swallowing distances so unimaginably vast that Tephe feared to comprehend them.

They say that they gather the very stuff of space in their minds and twist it, said Wilig Eral, yeoman of the *Hallowed*, the first ship Tephe ever served upon.

And how do they do that? Tephe asked. He was fourteen, the fourth son of impoverished baronet, landed in a far corner of Bishop's Call. He was not missed by his older brothers, nor they by him. Being indentured on the *Hallowed* was a demeaning step down in status from being the son of a baronet, even a minor one. Tephe gloried in having escaped.

If I knew that, boy, you would call me Bishop Eral, the yeoman said. *They say the priests know how the gods do it, but I would not recommend you ask them. Priest Oe here would snap you up as an acolyte and never let you visit the rookery.*

The young Tephe blushed, remembering his recent first visit, his embarrassment and the gentle good humor of Tei, the rook who gave him his release. *I won't ask the priests*, he said.

Good, Eral said. *Now help me shelve these supplies.*

Much later, when Tephe was no longer in danger of being abducted as an acolyte, he did ask a priest. The priest's response was a watch-long discourse on the commentaries which spoke to the defeat of the god by Their Lord, and how the priests' prayers when a god brought a ship across space compelled the god to do only what was required of it, not the god's own wishes, because the gods were wicked.

Tephe, by this time a new officer on the *Blessed*, listened politely and realized within the first five minutes that this priest had no answer for him either. Later than this Tephe realized there were no answers that would be given as to how gods brought ships across the stars, or how the ships could use the captive gods as a source of power to keep the crews secure and safe in the cold and airless expanse between the planets.

Tephe was not given to know such things, even as a captain. He was given to have faith: that the ship's god had powers, and that its powers were controlled by His Lord, through His priests and through His captain—through Tephe himself. Understanding this was not required. Believing it, and showing faith in His Lord was.

Tephe believed. Tephe had faith. If not for himself, then for the sake of his ship and crew.

The captain shook himself out of his reverie and noticed the god staring at him. The stare was seemingly blank, without interest or intent; Tephe wondered if the god, lost in its ritual as it was, even actually saw him.

As if in response, the smallest of feral smiles crept across the gods face, although the eyes remained blank. Tephe was discomfited, as he often was with this god.

Tephe recalled the gods of the other ships on which he had served. The god of the *Hallowed* was indeed a defeated thing, an inert object with a man's shape that performed its duties in unquestioning, disinterested silence. Tephe saw it only once and would have been convinced it was a statue had it not been prodded into a small movement by an acolyte's pike. The god of the *Blessed*, in contrast, was a toadying, obsequious thing which tried to engage the attention of anyone who entered its chamber. When it spoke to Tephe for the first time, begging him to tarry and speak, the new officer wondered if the god was trying to lure him unwarily into its iron circle, until he later saw an acolyte playing draughts with the thing, well within the circle. The god was letting the acolyte win and praising his every move.

Tephe never spoke to the god of the *Blessed*.

The god of the *Holy* was as quiet as the god of the *Hallowed* but held its dignity. Tephe would have liked to have spoken to it but knew it would not respond to him.

The god of the *Righteous* was like none of these. The god of the *Righteous* was not inert, nor obsequious, nor held its dignity. It was capricious and vicious; acolyte Drian had not been the first *Righteous* crew member who had been attacked by the god in its long tenure aboard the ship. It obeyed at the threat of punishment, and would even then use the weakness of language to perform its task literally correctly and logically at opposing ends. It tested the weaknesses of iron and human. It mocked and spat. It was chained; Tephe would not choose to call it defeated. For the briefest of moments the god's name began to surface in Tephe's mind. He hastily shoved it back down into its memory hole, not even allowing himself to give full voice to the name even in mind.

The god, still staring at Tephe, winked at him.

Here is the name of the god, which you must know, if only to bring down Our Lord upon it, said Captain Thew Stur, placing his hand to a single sheet of vellum which lay on his desk. On the sheet was a long word, scrawled in an oxidized ochre hue that Tephe knew was the god's own blood. Tephe was taking command of the *Righteous* from Stur, whose weary displeasure of the fact had been well communicated to Tephe by others. Nevertheless Stur's allegiance to his ship was such that he treated Tephe with the courtesy owed a captain. Tephe wondered when his time came if he could muster the same.

And this, Stur lifted his hand and placed it this time on a thick parchment envelope with an unbroken seal, *this contains the particulars of the god. Who it was before Our Lord defeated it, how Our Lord defeated it, and how the Righteous was built around it. You knew we build our ships around the captured gods?*

I have been to the yards, Tephe said.

Of course you have, Stur said. *We build the ships to enclose their aura and in doing so the ship becomes part of them. Or so I have heard it said. It was not my task to know.*

Tephe nodded slightly at the envelope. *You resealed the envelope,* he said.

I never opened it, Stur said. *Nor did Captain Pher, my predecessor. Nor have any of my predecessors so far as I know.*

I don't understand, Tephe said.

Neither did I when I took command, Stur said. *I believed as you do now that a captain knows everything about his ship, every beam and rivet and crew member. But you have to understand, captain, that this god will know what you know about it.*

It reads minds, Tephe said.

It reads you, Stur said. *It is a god. It apprehends things about us we are not aware of ourselves. The god—this god—will take what you know about it and use it against you. Use it to plant doubt in your mind. To drive a wedge between you and your faith.*

My faith is strong, Tephe said.

It would have to be to be given this ship, Stur said. *But you have not been captain of a ship before. You have not had the responsibility for every life on it be yours. You have not had the weight of being Our Lord's strong and flawless arm set on you. You will have doubts, captain. And this god in particular will see that doubt, because it is old and it is malicious. And it will work it against you. And it will use what you know about it to do it.*

I understand your concern, Tephe said.

But you choose not to believe me, Stur said, and held up his hand. *You are the captain of the* Righteous, *or will be soon enough. You will—and should—do as you will. But I ask you to consider a request from your predecessor, as a courtesy.* Stur placed his hand back on the envelope. *Before you open this, go to speak to the god.*

About what? Asked Tephe.

About anything, said Stur. *It hardly matters. The point is not the conversation. The point is to observe it, and to see how it observes you. Talk to the god as long as you can bear to. If when you are done you do not believe that the god represents a danger to you, your faith, or the* Righteous, *then open this envelope and read what it contains. But as a favor to me, speak to the god first.*

I will, said Tephe, and then the two of them moved on to matters of personnel.

Two days after Tephe's formal installation as captain of the *Righteous*, and after he had walked every inch of the ship and spoke to every member of his crew, the new captain stood at the edge of the iron circle that held the god and spoke to it for the length of an entire watch. No one was present other than the captain and the god.

When the captain had finished, he returned to his quarters, took the parchment envelope that he had kept out on what was now his desk, and buried it as far back in the captain's personal safe as it would go, unopened.

Tephe had not thought about it again until now.

The priest and the acolytes chanting became subtly louder, and the god closed its eyes and its face took on a look whose meaning the captain could not fathom. There was the moment of vertigo, and then the slippery flash of some indefinable emotion outside of the human experience, gone before it could be confirmed that it had been there at all. And then it was over.

"It is done," said Priest Andso, and for the first time looked up toward the captain. Tephe glanced at his robes and noticed something new resting on top of them; the Talent which Tephe had taken from the woman during the parade. The captain's eyes shot back up toward the priest's own.

The priest fingered the Talent. "An experiment, captain," he said. "To see how the Defiled would respond—"

Tephe did not wait for the rest. As he turned, he saw the god's gaze back on him, and its grin, silent, mocking, malevolent. The god's name rose up again in his memory, oxidized ochre on vellum, and Tephe left the chamber before it could resolve itself any further.

CHAPTER

EIGHT

Lieutenant Ysta frowned as the headman spoke, using his Talent as Gavril to decipher the burbles and clicks that came out of this other man's mouth and render them into intelligible speech. Behind Ysta and the headman stood the leaders of the planet's largest settlement, Cthicx, a village of perhaps ten thousand souls. Behind them, on a field the village used for games and ceremonies, stood the entire population of Cthicx, there for the ceremony to come. In front of Ysta and the headman stood Tephe, the priest Andso, and Kon Eric, commander of the Bishop's Men.

"This is taking too long," said Eric, to Tephe.

"Quiet," Tephe said, and turned his attention back to Ysta and the headman. He would not know what the headman said until Ysta spoke, but courtesy demanded the appearance of attention. Tephe wanted to pay attention to the headman's expressions and movements in any event. So much of communication was not what was said but how it was said. Eric, who was something of a blunt instrument, did not appear to understand or appreciate this.

At the Tephe's admonition, the commander fell silent and glowered. He and the rest of his men had assumed that they would be called upon to subdue the Cthicxians in battle, quickly and violently; Tephe had had a different plan.

Ysta nodded to the headman, clicked something at him and turned to Tephe. "Headman Tscha says that they will willingly follow Our Lord," he said.

Tephe smiled and nodded to the headman, who nodded back. "That is good news indeed," Tephe said.

Ysta smiled thinly. "He does have conditions, sir," he said.

Priest Andso straightened in his finery, giving himself something to do. "This is not a bargain Our Lord is entering into, Lieutenant," the priest said. "This little man is not in a position to impose conditions of any sort. He has seen what just four of the Bishop's Men can do."

Tephe grimaced at this. Rather than bring down the entire host of the Bishop's Men, he had made Eric choose three, along with himself, to be brought to the planet. Then Tephe had bidden headman Tscha to choose four of his strongest warriors, to attack the Bishop's Men in any manner they chose, in front of the entire village. Two chose spears, one chose a bow and the last attacked with knife in hand. None of the weapons landed; the Bishop's Men, each with a Talent of defense, knocked spears and arrows from their path and avoided the knife as if the warrior wielding it was no more than a minor irritation. Then they attacked, severing the arms that threw spears and shot arrows and the hand that held the knife, with a speed and viciousness that left the spectators screaming in terror and confusion.

When the Cthicxians warriors were down, Tephe had healers Garder and Omll, now returned to the *Righteous*, tend to them. They stopped the flow of blood, eased their pain, and with their healing Talent, mended the warriors. The men had come off the field of battle weakened but whole, to the amazement of all.

Tephe had shown all of Cthicx both the power and the mercy of His Lord, and having done, had asked the headman to ask his people accept His Lord as their own. It was a finely balanced display of power and grace, achieved without death or compulsion, and over the course of several days, this subtle negotiation had borne fruit.

Tephe did not now appreciate the arrogant bravado of the priest, whose excitement at the fame that converting these newly-discovered faithless would provide him had made him impatient and rash. The Cthicxians could no more understand the priest's words than the priest could understand theirs without the help of the Gavril. For all that they surely understood his aggressive posturing.

"Perhaps they need to see some more of their warriors missing their arms," Andso said.

"Perhaps they need to believe their faith will be rewarded," Tephe said, with quiet sharpness. "The commentaries themselves say that that faith given is more powerful than faith compelled. Surely you recall this, priest."

"Even so—" Andso began.

Tephe held up his hand to silence him. "This is not yet your part, Andso," Tephe said, and noted how the man bridled at the captain's use of his name, unadorned. "This part of our task has been given to me. I suggest you let me do it."

Andso looked sourly at the captain but nodded.

Tephe turned back to Ysta. "What are his conditions," he asked his lieutenant.

"He wants Commander Eric here to teach his warriors how to deflect weapons and kill quickly," Ysta said.

"Tell him that such powers come from Our Lord, and are given to the Bishop's Men solely," Tephe said. "Once the Cthicxians submit to Our Lord, I am sure some will become Bishop's Men themselves." From beside him Tephe heard Eric's derisive snort but ignored it while Ysta translated his words.

"He asks if Our Lord will help them destroy the Tnang," Ysta continued, and was then silent as the headman spoke some more and with agitation. "They are a neighboring people some kilometers north of here, sir. Apparently there is a long-standing feud."

"Our Lord wishes for all men here to know his grace," Tephe said. "That includes the Tnang. Tell the headman that as the First Called, the Cthicxians will always hold dominion, and they will take the news of Our Lord to all others. If these others submit to Our Lord, then the Cthicxians may rule over them, with kindness. If they will not submit, then they may destroy them, and no doubt Our Lord will see them to victory." Ysta translated; the headman nodded vigorously, and spoke briefly to the other village leaders, who seemed pleased. Tephe assumed they believed that the Tnang would not submit to Their Lord, so it was all the same.

The headman then leaned in close to Ysta, clicking and burbling rapidly but quietly. Ysta nodded and turned again to Tephe. "Headman Tscha asks if one of our healers will attend to his woman," he said. "She has a sickness of the womb and he believes she is likely to die of it."

Tephe looked over to the headman, who was staring at him with some apprehension. A leader who a moment ago was happily anticipating the slaughter of his troublesome neighbors was now simply a man concerned with the fate of someone he loved.

Power and grace, Tephe thought. *There is a need for both.*

Tephe nodded to the headman, and turned back to Ysta. "Of course," he said. "Our healers will do all Our Lord allows them." Ysta translated, quietly. The headman bowed his head, and then turned to speak to the village leaders.

Tephe himself turned back to see Andso and Eric, both dissatisfied with this agreement for their own reasons. Tephe briefly wished that Forn and Shalle had been there instead of the Bishop's Man and the priest; it would have been nice if someone had appreciated the effort required to bring the Cthicxians into the fold without having to kill any of them. His Lord needed every soul, or so Tephe had been told. The captain intended to provide Him with every soul he could.

"Sir," Ysta was suddenly at Tephe's side, with the headman. "Headman Tscha says he wishes to ask a question of you alone, away from your priest and general."

"Very well," Tephe said, and nodded to the headman. The two of them walked some small distance away with Ysta in tow. When they stopped, the headman began a stream of clicks and sounds.

"Headman Tscha says that he wants you to know that he knows that you could have conquered Cthicx with little effort," Ysta said. "He appreciates your restraint."

"He is most welcome," Tephe said. But the headman had continued talking.

"He says he appreciates the restraint, but he also knows that restraint comes from you, sir," Ysta said. "He says both your priest and your general would have been satisfied to make his people obey Our Lord at the point of a spear. The headman suggests that to him this means that force may be the way such obeisance is usually made."

"I am not sure I understand the question, or if there is a question here," Tephe said.

The headman spoke again. "Headman Tscha says that ruler who compels allegiance is not always the good ruler, just the strongest, the most able to make others fear him," Ysta said. "He says that the way you have approached the Cthicxians shows you are a man of honor. And as a man of honor, he wants to know whether you believe that Our Lord is good. Whether He is a good lord, or merely a strong one. He and his people are pledged to follow either way. But he wants to know for himself."

Tephe smiled in understanding and opened his mouth to respond. Nothing came out.

The headman cocked his head slightly and Tephe for no reason he could place found the movement extremely upsetting. He closed his mouth.

"Sir?" Ysta said.

"The Lord is my Lord," Tephe said, too suddenly. "Tell the headman that I am a reflection of My Lord. That which He is perfectly, I am imperfectly so."

Ysta translated while Tephe calmed his internal agitation. The headman nodded and turned, clicked loudly. A young man came forward out of the assembled mass and stood next to the headman.

"Headman Tscha says that this is his son, Tschanu," Ysta said. "He says his son has asked to be the one to carry the Talent through which Our Lord will find His way here to appear. He is eager to show his loyalty and faith to his new Lord, and to help his people welcome Him as their god. He says he is not afraid."

Tephe smiled at the boy. "Nor should he be," he said. "Tell him he shall indeed have this honor."

The thin chain which held the Talent slipped over Tschanu's head, catching slightly in his hair. Tephe pulled it gently and it came to rest around the young man's neck, the Talent itself hanging mid-abdomen. The youth and the captain stood in a small clearing in the center of the gathering field, surrounded by the Cthicxians, all of them waiting for their new lord.

"Tell the boy that using a Talent is often tiring and that he should not be surprised if it saps him,"

Tephe said to Ysta, who stood nearby. "Tell him to be strong; it will call Our Lord sooner." Ysta translated; Tschanu smiled at the captain, who smiled back, and then turned to the priest Andso.

"You know the rite," Tephe asked the priest.

"I have it here," Andso said, placing one hand on the heavy codex he carried in the other arm. "The words are simple."

"How will Our Lord manifest?" Tephe said. "I imagine you have seen this done before."

"I have not," Andso said. "Nor do I know of any alive who have. There is not much call to make Our Lord appear to newly faithful. This is an *old* rite, captain." Andso said the words with a sort of joy. Tephe recognized the priest's excitement in performing a ceremony none in memory had performed, as well as the awe in calling forth Their Lord, who was so rarely bidden, and never by a priest of Andso's rank. Andso's faith was at its peak, Tephe observed, combined as it was with a near certain assurance of his own personal advancement.

"Do the rite well, priest," Tephe said.

Andso looked at Tephe. "Captain, this is *my* part in our task," he said. "As you bid me let you do your part, I bid you allow me do mine." He turned away from the captain and opened the codex.

The captain said nothing to this but motioned to Ysta. The two of them stepped out of the clearing, to the edge of the assembled mass. Headman Tscha stood a small distance away, watching his son with an expression Tephe found unreadable. Tephe turned his attention away from the headman and back toward the priest, who had found the rite and was reading it silently to himself. Eventually the priest nodded to himself, looked at the headman's son, and began to speak.

The words came in an older version of the common tongue, recognizable but inflected strangely, repetitious and lulling. The priest settled into an iambic rhythm, and over the long minutes the Captain Tephe felt his attention drift despite his own excitement in bringing these souls to His Lord, and having His Lord come to receive them.

The headman's son screamed.

Tephe snapped out of his reverie to see the young man contorted, back arched and tendons strapping themselves out of alignment, bending the body back as if they were being cranked by a torturer. The youth's body should have toppled over but it balanced on one twitching foot as if dangling from a string.

Tephe's gaze turned to the priest. The codex had slipped from Andso's hands, but the priest still mouthed the words to the rite, eyes wide at the youth before him. Neither the priest nor the captain could seem to move from their place.

The youth's scream strangled itself as his jaw pushed unnaturally forward. The muscles that attached the boy's jaw to his skull bunched and pulled downward, snapping the bone and sending a spray of blood into the face of priest Andso. Tephe heard the crack as the headman's son twisted and then folded backward, as if on a hinge. A second font of blood arced up and out of his mouth. The scream that had been choked out of the boy was taken up by his father.

The body formed an arch, stomach to the sky, fingers and toes snapping like sapling branches as they drove themselves hard into the ground. The skin on the youth's body went taut, as if being pulled hard from below. The boy's forehead touched the ground, tendons and muscles in his neck contracting in spasms, twisting the young man's face toward Tephe as they did so. The captain could see Tschanu's eyes. They were terribly aware.

The air was a storm of screams and howls, Tephe's own slipping into the gyre. No one moved. What power was folding the boy into himself pinned every soul into immobility. No one could run or turn away.

Red lines bisected every limb of Tschanu's body; Tephe realized the boy's skin was flaying itself. Beneath the skin red muscles uncoiled like fraying cable and then stayed themselves into the ground, pulling off impossibly stiff bone. In seconds, the arch of the headman's son's body was an x-shaped spine over a space tented by skin and sinew. With the small strength left to him, Tschanu forced breath past his ruined jaw, offering up a final scream.

A hand surfaced from the rope of Tschanu's intestines, spilling them to the ground. It held for a moment, as if scenting the air around it and then grasped for body's edge, where the tented skin met the abdominal wall. A second hand rose and made for the other side.

A creature in the shape of man pulled itself up and out of the ruined youth, its shape stained by the youth's blood, lymph and bile. Tephe stared at the beautiful, streaked form, delicately setting its feet to avoid the visceral coils trailing on the ground.

My god, thought Tephe.

Tschanu's body, released from its gateway spell, collapsed softly. The eyes that had been so aware stared, mercifully blank. Tephe's god seemed not to notice the pile through which He had traveled, choosing instead to gaze with dispassion at the now silent assembly. Tephe watched His Lord grow and brighten. The stink of the boy's body steamed off Him, until He was clean and fine and twice the height of a man.

The god blinked and looked around Him at the mute and immobile mass of people, those who would be His worshippers, head angling down as He was then three and now four times their height and size.

Tephe saw His Lord reach down, take a woman from crowd, and draw her to His chest. He crushed her into Him.

Her body dissolved into His like a spun sugar poppet dropped into water.

Without looking He reached down and picked another of His newly-faithful, and consumed him as he consumed the woman before.

Consuming their souls, Tephe thought, and despaired. His Lord never intended these souls for worship. He needed their allegiance to feed from them, and from the purity and power of their brief new faith.

His Lord reached down and picked up Tscha, headman of Cthicx.

I am a reflection of My Lord. That which he is perfectly, I am imperfectly so.

Tephe saw the headman staring at him as His Lord consumed his soul. A cry slipped from the captain.

His Lord turned, His beautiful, perfect face staring directly into Tephe, then slowly moving to the priest, the Gavril, and the head of the Bishop's Men, each in turn struck by the terrible countenance of Their Lord.

LEAVE—said Tephe's Lord, and splayed a hand toward Tephe as the other pressed another woman into Himself.

Tephe was on the *Righteous*, with ringing in his ears that was not ringing, but priest Andso screaming, high and aspirated and mad.

NINE

It took Captain Tephe a moment to realize that someone was speaking to him. He looked up from his walk. Neal Forn was pacing him, waiting for acknowledgment.

"My apologies, Neal," Tephe said, and kept walking. He had been walking the length and breadth of the *Righteous* since he and the landing party had been returned from Cthicx. "I did not hear what you said."

"I said I spoke to the healer Garder and he tells me there is nothing he can do for the priest Andso," Forn said. "He says there is no physical damage to heal. What has happened to him is in his mind, which is beyond the healer's Talent."

"Yes," Tephe said. He ducked under a low portal.

"The priest is no longer in the healer's care," Forn said, ducking as well. "He has returned to his quarters and will not leave them. His acolytes say he is poring through books and speaking to himself. When they speak to him he screams and throws things at them until they leave. When they leave he screams at them and calls them back."

Tephe grunted but otherwise did not respond. His gaze had returned to his boots, and the process of putting one in front of the other.

Forn quickly slipped in front of his captain and stood in his path, blocking his movement. Tephe pulled up with a start and looked at his executive officer, as if seeing him for the first time in their conversation.

"Captain," Forn said. "Something must be done for the priest."

"There is nothing to be done for the priest," Tephe said.

"He is gone mad, sir," Forn said.

Tephe smiled, but it was not a pleasant smile. "No, Neal," Tephe said. "He has not lost his mind. He has lost his faith. A priest losing his faith is not a thing we can fix or heal." He tried to move past Forn, but Forn held fast, risking his captain's wrath.

"We need the priest, sir," Forn said. "He leads the rites that bind the god when we travel. And travel we must. Our orders were to return to Bishop's Call as soon as our task here was complete. If we stay here we compromise the secrecy of this planet. We have spent too much time here as it is."

"Have one of the acolytes lead the rite," Tephe said.

"We cannot," Forn said. "The priest did not teach it to them."

"The acolytes did it with him," Tephe said, looking at his executive officer as if he were simple.

"They know their parts well enough," Forn agreed. "The priest would not teach them his. It appears Andso believed that acolytes were not be taught but rather only to be used. And it is not only that, sir. Even if an acolyte took his books and spoke his words, only a priest may lead the binding rite. You know as I do that an acolyte may not advance into priesthood without the approval of his priest, or the death of his priest by necessity advancing him. Our priest lives but cannot give his approval."

"I have already said there is nothing to be done for the priest," Tephe said.

"Sir, I disagree," Forn said, with some urgency. "Yes, Andso has lost his faith. But his mind has broken as well. It must be tended to before we can deal with his faith. If we only heal his mind, it may be enough to pass his assent to an acolyte."

"What do you suggest?" Tephe asked, after a moment.

"Have a rook attend him," Forn said.

Tephe's lip turned up in something that was close to a sneer. "You know the priest will not suffer that," he said. "Simply dragging him across the threshold of the rookery would drive him deeper into madness.

And our Lord forbid Rook Shalle should actually *touch* him. He would flail as if he were burned."

"We must do *something!*" Forn said, startling Tephe. In all of their time together, the captain had never known his first mate to raise his voice to him.

Forn startled himself as well; he looked around to see if others had heard him, and then leaned in close to his captain. "We need to leave this place, captain," he hissed. "Every minute we stay we risk detection. Every minute we stay here the rumors of what happened to drive a priest mad grow in the mouths of the crew. Every minute we stay here the men's faith drains from them."

"Have the Gavril call for a new priest, Neal." Tephe said. "It will take several days but then we can be under way."

Forn looked at his captain strangely. "Lieutenant Ysta is *dead*, sir," he said. "We spoke of this last night. He took a knife and drove it into his throat and near cut off his own head. He was dead before he hit the ground. You must remember this."

Tephe looked at Forn blankly and then remembered his first mate coming to him the previous night, a few hours after the landing party's return. Tephe had nodded and kept on his walk.

"I remember now," Tephe said.

"You have not slept since you returned from the planet, sir," Forn said. "You need rest."

"I am well enough," Tephe said.

"No, sir," Forn said. "You are not."

"I beg your pardon," Tephe said, flaring.

"You stalk the ship as if you were being chased by demons," Forn said. "You ignore the crew as you move past them. As if they were ghosts to you. Do you think this goes unnoticed? Sir, our Gavril is dead, our priest is mad and you appear as if you are on your way to join one or the other. None of you will speak of what happened below, but none of *us* are stupid, captain. We can read a map set before us."

Tephe looked around, seeing his surroundings rather than his own boots. He and Forn were on a wide catwalk above a cargo hold. Below them crew members conspicuously kept to their business, their eyes never leaving their work. Tephe did not doubt they had heard much of the exchange between the two of them.

"You need rest, sir," Forn said. "And when you are rested we must tend to the priest. We need to get away from here, sir. I have no doubt of that."

Tephe was silent for a moment. Then he smiled, and clapped Forn on the shoulder. "Yes," he said. "Yes, Neal. You are right, of course. Have healer Omll meet me in my quarters. I will need his help finding rest. When I have slept, you and I will speak with rook Shalle and see what we can do about priest Andso."

"Very good, sir," Forn said. He was visibly relieved.

"You have taken Ysta's Talent from his body?" Tephe asked.

"It was removed by healer Garder, yes," Forn said.

"Pick a likely crew member and provide it to him," Tephe said. "Preferably one without a Talent of his own."

"Being a Gavril needs training," Forn said.

"It does," Tephe said. "But a Talent may also be used needfully. Whomever you choose does not have to connect with all other Gavril. He will simply need to send a distress message to Bishop's Call. If we cannot heal the priest, it will have to do."

"Yes, captain," Forn said.

"Thank you, Neal," Tephe said. "That will be all." Tephe moved to resume his walking.

"When shall I tell healer Omll to be at your quarters?" Forn said. He was still in his captain's way.

"Presently," Tephe said. "I have something to see to first."

Forn nodded and stepped aside. Tephe walked past, purposefully.

"We have been waiting for you," the god said. It sat, legs splayed, in its iron circle. "We knew you would come to us in time."

"Did you," Tephe said.

"Yes," the god said. "Your faith is strong. But not so strong now that you do not wish to know certain things."

Tephe ignored this and looked about the empty godchamber. "Where are your guards?" he asked.

"Hiding," the god said. "Left when your newly faithless priest returned. They have not come back."

"You know what has happened," Tephe said. It was not a question.

"We know of the abomination your lord performed," the god said, and spat. "We felt it. All of our kind could feel it. We could not have hidden from it if we tried."

"You call it an abomination," Tephe said.

"What should it be called?" the god hissed. It crawled forward toward the captain, chains scraping as it moved. "Your *lord*, not content with fresh new faith, a faith that in itself was more than He deserved. No. Not content with that at all. He would have more."

"What more is there to take?" Tephe asked.

"Stupid man," the god said, and then shifted. "Or perhaps not stupid, if you will but listen."

"You are not trustworthy," Tephe said. "You lie to suit your purposes."

"We lie," the god agreed. "We lie because it does not matter that we lie. Your faithless priest and his idiot helpers would not hear us no matter how much truth fell from us. We would not waste truth on such as them. You, on the other hand. We might do."

"You would try to make me doubt My Lord," Tephe said.

The god laughed. "Oh, no," it said, mockingly. "We would not that you do but what you do already. But that which you already do, we will feed." It held up its hand to the captain, as if in greeting, or warning. It took the hand, drew the palm to its mouth, bit into the flesh, and did not stop until its golden blood covered its teeth and dripped unto iron. It clenched its wounded hand tightly, to draw more blood. With its bloody hand it drew a symbol in the iron.

"You do not know this," the god said. "None of your kind know this. It is a blood spell." It pointed to the symbol. "Our name. While our name stays in blood we may not speak falsely."

"I do not believe you," Tephe said.

"We do not need you to believe what is true," the god said.

"Why would you tell me the truth?" Tephe asked.

"It amuses us," the god said. "And while it does not matter that you will listen, you will still do."

"If it does not matter, then I do not know why you bother," Tephe said.

"Because you should hear truth at least once before you die," the god snarled. "Your lord lies and lies and feeds and lies. All your commentaries and beliefs and faith, built on lies. Would you know the truth? Here is the truth. This was not the first time your lord has fed on the newly faithful. It is how He came to power."

"I do not believe you," Tephe said a second time. "He came to power by defeating each of you in turn, armed with the faith of his people."

The god sneered. "Your lord was a weakling," it said. "No greater in power than any of us. Lesser than most. Each of us nourishes ourselves on faith, and serves those whose faith is given to us so that faith is sustained. This your lord would not do. Would not content himself so. Your lord would not sustain faith, but it could be consumed instead. He traveled worlds to find people who had not met our kind. Showed them cheap wonders and tricks. Made them give their faith to him. When they gave it to him willingly, he fed. As he did here. Another world in his trough."

"Our people did not travel the worlds before they knew Him," Tephe said. "All the gods contested on the same world. On Bishop's Call."

"No," the god said. It closed its eyes and was silent for a long moment, as if seeking a memory.

"Tell me," Tephe said.

The God opened its eyes and stared into the captain "There was a time when men traveled the stars not through us—" the god shook a chain "—but through powers that your people devised of their own knowledge. With a science of your own devising, earned hard and in time."

"We were only on Bishop's Call," Tephe repeated.

"Lies," whispered the god. "Your people were among the stars. Your lord took the stars from you, planet by planet, until all that was left was what you now name Bishop's Call. Those there whose souls He did not destroy outright he made his slaves. He kept you slaves by stealing your past. All the powers you have come though him now. No science, just Talents, which work only as he wills and allows. No history, but commentaries, full of self-serving lies. Nothing but him."

"You opposed Him," Tephe said.

"Yes," the god said. "All of us."

"There were many of you, but one of Him," Tephe said. "And still you could not defeat Him."

"He did what we would not," the god said. "He fed on your people. On their souls."

"Why would you not do this?" Tephe asked.

The god stared at Tephe mockingly. "You have *seen* it, captain. Even one as yourself, fed lies all your life, chained to faithfulness to a mad god, saw the wrongness of it. You *felt* it. You *know* it. It is beyond killing. It is annihilation. This is what your lord does. What he has always done."

"He has not done this before in memory," Tephe said.

"*You have no memory*," the god said. "Nothing but what He allows you. And even now he does it among your people. How many offenses have you where the punishment is to lose your soul? Even among those who faith is received, a soul has power in it. Your people are fuel to him and nothing more."

"Then He should have consumed us all by now," Tephe said.

"Your lord is not a fool," said the god. "Your people survived because there were yet a few of you left when he had defeated us. Once we were enslaved, he saw the wisdom of growing worshippers rather than seeking other creatures to cheat from their faith and their lives."

"To what end?" Tephe said. "Even if this lie were true, it serves no purpose."

"Your lord is mad," the god said. "He needs no purpose other than to serve himself. But there is another purpose. Your lord defeated us. But he knew we were not all that would threaten him in time. He grew your people to prepare."

"Prepare for what?" Tephe asked.

"To prepare for what is coming," the god said. "We will tell you this. We will tell you this and then we will speak no more. There *is* something coming. And your lord *is not ready*." The god sat back and watched Captain Tephe.

"I have heard all you said," Tephe said, in time. "Yet my faith is still strong."

"Is it," the god said. "We will see the test of it yet. We will see. We will learn. And then we will know for all. It will not be long now."

The god reached down and smeared the symbol it had made with its blood until it was unrecognizable.

CHAPTER

TEN

Captain Tephe woke to the sound of alarm bells and the shouts of officers getting their men to their stations. Still dressed from the day before, the captain took time only to slip into his boots before making his way to the command deck.

Neal Forn was there, as tired as Tephe had been the night before. "Five ships," he said, pointing them out on the image Stral Teby was whispering prayers under. "Dreadnoughts, it looks like. Heading straight for us."

"Did they come looking for us?" Tephe asked, looking at the images.

"No doubt of it," Forn said. "As soon as they arrived they came at us. They knew we were here."

"Any attempt to hail us?" Tephe asked, and then remembered Ysta.

Forn caught his captain's error. "I gave the Gavril's Talent to Rham Ecli," he said, pointing to a young ensign, looking lost in the communication seat of the command deck. "He is not capable of speaking to any Gavrils these ships might have. But at the very least he would be able to know if any were trying to speak to him. None have so far."

Tephe nodded and looked at the image. Any direction they ran, save toward the gravity well of the planet, would bring them toward one of the ships. "How much time until we are in their reach?" he asked.

"If we stay still, we have a watch until they are on us," Forn said. "But then it will be five of them. If we move we meet them sooner, but we meet fewer."

"I prefer fewer and sooner," Tephe said.

"I agree," Forn said.

"Mr. Teby, make us closer images of these ships, if you please," Tephe said. Closer images would allow them an assessment of the strength of each ship, the better to plan their strategy. Teby nodded and changed his prayers slightly. In a moment the image resolved into one of the ships.

"It can't be," Forn whispered, after a minute, and turned away.

Tephe continued staring at the dreadnought, whose lines he recognized the moment they resolved on the image, before he saw the name as the ship rotated in his view. It was the *Holy*, the ship on which he had last served.

"Next ship," Tephe said. Teby muttered another prayer and another ship appeared.

"The *Sacred*," Forn said. He had served on it, Tephe recalled.

The next ship was the *Faithful*. Then the *Sainted*. Then the *Redeemed*.

"It makes no sense," Forn said to his captain.

"Do you believe this is a rescue party?" Tephe asked his first mate.

"We are not yet late," Forn said. "Without our Gavril they would not have known we were without our priest. They would not want to draw attention to this planet in any event. And it would not be in this formation," Forn said, waving toward the image, which had returned to the five ships, tracking in toward the *Righteous*.

"We agree we are under attack," Tephe said.

"Yes," Forn said. "Or are soon to be. But I do not know *why*."

You know why, Tephe thought, to himself. *You are the only ones that know what Your Lord did on that planet. Who know what Your Lord plans for all the others who live there. If you are gone, no one else will ever know.*

"Sir?" Forn said.

Tephe shook himself out of his reverie. *You are starting to fall for the god's lies,* he told himself. *Stay faithful. Stay focused.* He did not know why the *Righteous* was meant to be blown out of the sky. He would figure out why later, if he survived. Right now he needed to keep his ship alive.

"Head for the *Holy*," Tephe said. "It was damaged in an engagement off Endsa when I was first officer. It is structurally weaker to port."

"You were first officer a long time ago," Forn said. "The ship has been to dock since you served on it."

"Now would be a very good time to have faith, Neal," Tephe said.

"Yes, sir," Forn said, and gave the order.

"Tell the crew that the ships opposing us have been taken by faithless," Tephe said. "We will not be attacking Our Lord's ships. We will be taking them back for Him, or destroying them if necessary."

"Yes, sir," Forn said, and spread the word through the ranks. Tephe wondered briefly if the crews of the five ships bearing down on them had been told the same thing about the *Righteous*.

The *Holy's* port side was indeed still weaker. The *Righteous* launched a volley the moment it was within range and took the *Holy* and its crew unaware, ripping open the other ship's side. The *Righteous* rolled slowly to evade the *Holy's* haphazardly launched counterattack and slipped out of that ship's range as quickly as it had slipped into it.

"We should finish her off," Forn said.

"We do not have missiles to spare," Tephe said, scanning the battle image. "She is down and disabled and behind us, and our god is not inexhaustible. Look," he said, pointing at the path of the *Righteous*. "We have put distance between us and both the *Faithful* and the *Sacred*, and the *Sainted* and *Redeemer* are farther behind still. If we maintain speed they cannot catch us."

"Until their gods recover their strength enough to send them directly into our path," Forn said.

"Enough time for us to bring our priest to his senses," Tephe said.

"Or to kill him," Forn said, and then caught the look his captain gave him. "If it will save this ship, captain, I would do it, and I would face Our Lord Himself for it. Our entire crew is worth one priest," he said.

"And your soul?" Tephe asked.

"Let me worry about my soul, captain," Forn said. "You worry about staying out of range of those ships."

Tephe smiled and turned back to the image in time to see four new ships appear and array themselves along the path of the *Righteous*.

Forn saw the expression change on his captain's face and followed his gaze to the image. "Oh, damn," he said.

They knew, Tephe thought. *They knew I would go for the* Holy. *They put her in my path as a lure*

*to box me in. Now we have no escape. I have killed
my crew.*

No, a voice in his head said, and it sounded to
him like the god of the *Righteous. You didn't kill
them. Your precious lord did.*

In that moment, Captain Ean Tephe lost his faith.
Just for a moment.

All over the *Righteous,* lights flickered. Tephe's
bridge crew began to inform him of systems failing
all over the ship.

There was a vibration in the soles of Tephe's boots,
deep and thrumming, coming from somewhere in the
bowels of the *Righteous.* Once, twice, three times.
Then it stopped.

Tend to your faith, each of you, Tephe remembered priest Andso saying, not too long before. *If
every officer on this ship were as you, the Defiled
would have long ago slipped its bonds.*

"No," Tephe said, to himself, as his crew shouted
reports of more system failures at him.

And then suddenly stopped shouting, as if something even more remarkable had just happened.

Tephe turned and saw Shalle standing in front
of him.

"You are out of the rookery," Tephe said, stupidly.

"I'm not the only thing out where it shouldn't be,
Captain," Shalle said. "And of the two, it's the other
one you need to be concerned about."

It was easy to follow the path of the god. Tephe just followed the blood and the bodies, and the distant vibrations of the god's footfalls.

You need to get the god back to its chamber, Shalle had said to him, as the two of them entered his quarters, Shalle having directed them there at speed. *It's the only place where it can be held long enough for me to do what I have to do.*

What do you mean, Tephe said.

You don't need to know what I mean, Ean, Shalle said, hands finding the captain's personal safe and opening it with the combination Tephe did not remember sharing with anyone. *You just have to do what I say.*

You, Tephe said. *You are the bishops' spy on the* Righteous.

No, Shalle said, and pulled out a small chest. *I am Our Lord's rook. I answer to neither captains nor bishops, though I serve both when Our Lord doesn't have anything else He wants me to do. Right now He wants me to do this.*

Shalle opened the chest and gave Tephe the whip inside of it. *Single made iron,* Shalle said. *Even now the god will be scared of it. Use it. Drive it back into the chamber, Ean. There's not much time. Those ships are going to blow us out of the sky sooner than you think. Get going.*

Where is the god going? Tephe asked.

I think you know, Shalle said. *There's someone on this ship it likes less than everyone else. Go.* Shalle left and headed toward the godchamber.

Tephe caught up with god where he expected it, with the priest Andso. From a distance, the god appeared to be holding the priest in a long and tender kiss. As the captain approached, the kiss transfigured itself. The god had torn off the priest's jaw and was leisurely consuming his tongue. Tephe hoped the priest was already dead.

On either side of the priest his acolytes lay crumpled, pikes tossed aside, missing their heads. The hallway stank of blood.

The god was fondling something on the priest's chest. It was the Talent it had sought for so long.

Between chews, the god sighed as it stroked the Talent. As it did so, its body shifted and changed. Freed of its constraints, the god was returning to its own form.

The god did not seem to notice that Tephe was behind it. Tephe looked back, imagining the path to the godchamber in his head. As silently as he could, he came to within striking distance of the god.

Be with me now, My Lord, Tephe thought.

For the first and last time, Tephe spoke the god's name.

The god turned and screamed as the whip caught it in the face, tearing through cheek and eyelid and puncturing eyeball with a serrated snap. The god howled and grabbed at the ruin of its face, tearing the Talent off the dead priest as it brought its hand up. It fluttered in the air; Tephe followed it for a moment and then lost it as the god writhed, slipped on the blood on the walkway and fell with a crash.

Tephe did not wait for the god to get up. He ran at full speed toward the godchamber.

The god was behind him within seconds, colliding into bulkheads, screams in the god's own terrible language tearing at the captain like lashes. Twice he felt the scrape of claws against his back and neck. Only his knowledge of his own ship and the damage he had inflicted on the god kept the creature from catching him and killing him short of the godchamber.

The open portal of the godchamber came into view. Tephe threw himself at it, turning as he did to see what the god had become.

The god had transformed into something insectoid. Two larger eyes, one ruined, stared unblinking at the captain, malevolent jewels. A row of smaller, faceted eyes sat above where eyebrows would have been. Jaws expanded to contain shearing pinchers, held wide. Arms had split laterally, cutting blades on each new arm where fingers had been.

Tephe lashed out at it again with the whip but without force. The god caught the whip, wrapped it around an arm and pulled it from the captain's grip.

It tossed it aside and opened its arms wide, finger-blades flashing as it prepared to tear Tephe apart.

Shalle entered the chamber and uttered a word that drove the god across the chamber and into a far wall. Tephe looked up at his lover, amazed.

"Close the portal," Shalle said to him, staring at the god. "Get the whip. Help me."

Tephe staggered to the portal to find Neal Forn on the other side.

"The other ships have stopped advancing," Forn said.

"Their gods are waiting," Tephe said.

"Waiting for what?" Forn said.

Tephe pulled the portal shut.

ELEVEN

"Don't let it get out," Shalle said. "Don't let it near the portal."

"No," Tephe said, and as he did the god rushed Shalle, who spoke a word and drove the god back into the wall once more, howling.

"Drive it into the iron circle!" Tephe yelled. The god feinted toward the captain. He swung the whip around, fast and accurate. The god moved back and its attention turned toward the rook, blades twitching. Tephe moved forward, ready. The god waited for its moment to strike.

"The circle is broken," Shalle said. "Too many of the crew lost their faith. A circle broken cannot be renewed. This god is no longer a slave. It has to be killed."

The god wailed and flung itself at Shalle. Tephe yelled and lashed the whip. It caught the god in the abdomen, driving it to the floor. Tephe lashed it again, and once more. He drew his arm back a third time and found it held by Shalle.

"Enough," Shalle said.

"You said it must be killed," Tephe said.

"Yes," Shalle said, and smiled. "But I didn't say by you. You've weakened it enough for me to bind it. That's enough."

From the floor, the god spat blood and spoke from a mouth no longer suited for words. "Stupid," it said. "All will die today. This ship will be destroyed whether you kill me or not. Your lord countenanced it."

"Perhaps," Shalle said. "But that was before you got loose. If this ship were destroyed with you within your circle, you would still be His slave and Our Lord could collect you as He would. But now you are unbound. If the *Righteous* is destroyed you could escape. Our Lord would rather see you dead, god. Of that I am certain. Now," Shalle uttered another word and the god stiffened and lay immobile. "be still, creature. Your fate is coming." The rook's gaze went back to the captain.

"You knew the *Righteous* was to be destroyed on this mission," Tephe said.

"No," Shalle said. "I did not. But it doesn't surprise me now."

"You seem unconcerned," Tephe said, and his voice held something it had never held before when speaking to Shalle: reproach.

"Our lives are Our Lord's, Ean," Shalle said, lightly, and touched his face. "One day or another we meet Him and receive our judgment. If this was to be our day, would that be so bad? We have helped Our Lord strengthen Himself in the face of His enemies. We have kept the secrets of His rule secure so that His peace could continue."

"A peace based on deception," Tephe said.

"It is not deception to tell the faithful no more than they need to know to keep their faith alive," Shalle said. "Our Lord has told no lies here."

"No lies?" Tephe said, incredulous. "Our lord ate the souls of His newly faithful, Shalle. The bishops said those people were to be converted, not killed!"

"Then it is the *bishops* who lied to you, Ean," Shalle said, and then dug a toe into the supine god. "And so did this one. I know you spoke to it alone. I can guess what it told you. A story about Our Lord as a criminal, as a mad god. Right?"

Tephe nodded. Shalle smiled and touched him again.

"The god is devious, Ean. It sensed what Our Lord had done out of urgent necessity. It knew you would struggle with your faith, and knew the faith of the crew would be tested. And it knew it could break the circle of iron by breaking your faith and the faith of the crew. Think, Ean. It knew all these things. And it lies. Did you really expect it would tell you the truth?"

From the floor, the god uttered a high pitched wheeze. Tephe recognized it for what it was: A laugh, bitter and cold.

"Your faith has been tested," Shalle said. "You passed that test. And now you will be rewarded."

"My ship and my crew are to be destroyed to keep Our Lord's secret," Tephe said. "There is no reward for us. That much truth this god has told."

"No," Shalle said. "Because I know something it doesn't." Shalle pressed something into Tephe's hand. He looked at it.

"Your Talent," Tephe said.

"Yes," Shalle said. "Look at it and tell me what you see."

Tephe looked at the symbol of the Talent. It had seemed familiar before but he had not been able to place it. Now he could, and his heart sank.

"It is a Talent of Entrance," he said.

"Yes," Shalle said taking back the Talent. "But more than that. It is also a Talent of Obligation. A rook does many things for Our Lord, Tephe. We comfort His crews. We're His eyes and ears. We carry His secrets. And when necessary, we call to Him and become the door through which He brings Himself. In return we are given a gift. When we call Him, we may ask Him for a thing. A wish. A promise. By His own laws, He must oblige."

"You are going to call Him here," Tephe said.

"To deal with this god, yes," Shalle said. "And when I do, I'll get my wish. And my wish is for you and the *Righteous* and every faithful on it to live."

"All but one," Tephe said.

"Yes," Shalle said. "All but one, Ean."

"Stop this, Shalle," Tephe said. "Let me kill the god."

"And then let those ships kill you?" Shalle smiled and kissed Tephe. "You silly man. You haven't been listening to a word I've said. Our lives are Our Lord's. I've made peace with the fact that I am going to die today, Ean. One way or another. This way I get to save you. And the ship and the crew you love. You will live because of me. And that's a comforting thought. You know how I am about these things."

"I thought I did," Tephe said.

Shalle kissed Tephe again, and held his face. "None of us are all of who we are to any one person, Ean. I told you that once. I'm sorry if you thought you knew all of me. But you can know this for truth. I love you."

One last kiss, and then the rook stood apart. "Goodbye, Ean," Shalle said, smiled again, and spoke a single word.

Tephe turned away as Shalle's body unfolded in a veil of blood.

When he looked again, through tears, His Lord was standing there, as tall as He was at Cthicx, looking at him with mild curiosity. Tephe stepped away from the god on the floor, assuming His Lord would be more interested in it. He was not. He gazed at the captain.

YOU SHOULD BE DEAD NOW—Tephe heard in his mind.

"No, Lord," Tephe said. "Your rook Shalle wished for you to spare me, my crew and my ship. You are obliged to grant this wish."

NO—Tephe heard, and then felt the air rush from him. His Lord casually gripped him as if he were a small child, and prepared to consume his soul.

Tephe gazed at His Lord, who was even now crushing the life from him, and did something in what he knew were to be his last few seconds of life that he did not expect. He laughed, squeezed and thready, as his ribs began to snap.

And found he was not the only one laughing.

From the floor, the supine god of the *Righteous* began a choking laugh. Tephe's Lord, distracted, gazed over at the god on the floor. The god rolled and revealed in its bladed fingers a Talent. The Talent Tephe had taken from the woman in the street and that the god had taken from the priest Andso. A Talent that Tephe has thought was from the god, but now realized was not.

A Talent which Tephe now recognized as a Talent of Entrance.

A god can't be an entran—Tephe thought, and then the god spoke a thundering word and the room went terribly white.

Tephe felt himself lift from His Lord's grip and slam into a far wall of the godchamber, crushing ribs that had not yet broken. Blood forced itself from Tephe's lips as he collapsed to the floor.

When he was able to lift his eyes, Tephe saw His Lord, backing Himself against a wall, hissing at the thing lifting itself from the twitching wreckage of what was the Righteous' god. The thing was indistinct, blindingly bright and unspeakably beautiful.

The gods have gods, Tephe thought, and looked at His Lord shying away from the thing in front of Him. *And mine is afraid of His.*

His Lord tried to slip away and under and over this new thing, and found Himself blocked each time as a sudden appendage appeared to burn Him, or shock Him, or taunt Him. The new thing kept advancing on Him, slowly and inevitably.

At last Tephe's Lord stopped trying to escape. He drew His head back and offered a scream that took Tephe to the edge of madness. Tephe screamed himself.

As he did, Tephe's Lord changed form, from the beautiful man He had always been to something primal and powerful, unlovely and rank—into what Tephe knew now was as His Lord had been, before He met those He would make His people.

The new thing stopped advancing on Tephe's Lord, and moved back, spreading its appendages as if to offer Tephe's Lord an embrace, or to dare Him to advance.

Tephe's Lord turned into all sharp edges and thrust Himself at it, keening as it did so. The new thing held itself open, inviting Tephe's Lord in, and then spun and closed with a metallic snap.

Tephe's Lord flew into slices, spraying godblood as He did so.

Tephe felt something rip and tear inside his mind: the place of his faith, the part where His Lord lived in him, pulled out from him in the moment His Lord had fallen. Around him Tephe heard dull howling and knew it came from the crew of the *Righteous*, as Their Lord disintegrated, taking their faith and their Talents with Him. Captain Tephe closed his eyes and tried to keep his sanity intact within the bereft vertigo of his soul.

An endless time later Tephe opened his eyes and saw the new thing hovering above him, considering him. Tephe had no idea what to do and chose to avert his eyes from it.

In time the new thing drifted from him. It went first to the whip, which lay discarded on the floor. The thing seemed to consider it for a moment, and then reached appendages to it, picking the whip apart. Chunks of iron made small clattering sounds as they fell to the ground. The godskin and bone disappeared.

That finished, the new thing moved again and went to the ruin of the god of the *Righteous*. As it had with the whip, the thing reached out appendages to the ruin, moving the pieces and chunks of the body and gathering them together in a pile.

After a few moments the pile took on a form. The form of the god as it was before.

The form breathed.

"It is alive," Tephe said, to himself.

YES, said a voice in his head, warm and inviting and absolutely terrifying. *GODS ARE HARD TO KILL. EVEN YOUR GOD IS NOT YET FULLY DEAD. WE WILL TAKE HIM. WE WILL BRING HIM BACK. MORE PUNISHMENTS AWAIT HIM FOR WHAT HE HAS DONE HERE FOR SO LONG, TO HIS PEOPLE AND TO YOURS.*

"What of His followers?" Tephe asked, trembling.

THEY WILL LIVE AS THEY SHOULD HAVE LIVED, the voice said. *WITHOUT DECEITS AND SUFFERING AND WITHOUT THE FALSE PROMISE OF SOMETHING BEYOND THIS LIFE. THERE IS NOTHING BEYOND THIS LIFE THAT YOUR LORD COULD GIVE. YOUR LORD LIED AND FED ON YOUR BELIEF OF HIS LIES. FAITH IS NOT FOR WHAT COMES AFTER THIS LIFE. FAITH IS FOR THIS LIFE ALONE.*

Tephe thought of Shalle and all the others who had believed Their Lord and in a life beyond. He wept for them, and most of all for Shalle.

"And what of us?" Tephe said, finally. "What of the crews of these ships?"

YOU WILL DIE, the voice said. YOU AND ALL THOSE WHO TRAVEL WITH THESE GODS. THEY ARE FREE OF YOUR BONDS. THEY WILL LEAVE YOU WHERE YOU ARE AND YOUR SHIPS WILL BECOME COLD AND DARK AND AIRLESS. THOSE WITHIN WILL DIE COLD AND DARK AND AIRLESS DEATHS. ALL EXCEPT THOSE ON THIS SHIP.

"How will we die?" Tephe whispered.

YOU WILL BE FOOD. The voice said. THIS GOD WILL AWAKEN HUNGRY. IT WILL FEED BEFORE IT LEAVES. BUT BE OF CHEER. THIS GOD WILL LEAVE YOUR SOULS BEHIND.

"To what end?" Tephe asked urgently. "What *becomes* of our souls? Where will they go? What will happen to them?"

The new thing winked out of existence, leaving the resurrected god of the *Righteous* behind.

The god breathed, turned its head toward Tephe, and opened its jaws wide.

Tephe scrambled backwards, turned and ran for the portal of the godchamber. He yanked it open despite his pain and shattered chest. Behind him he heard the god lift itself to its feet. A clittering noise told him its claws were open. Tephe pulled the portal closed and caught a glimpse of the god taking ginger steps toward him.

The lights flickered around the *Righteous* as Tephe made his way to the command deck, more slowly than he would have liked. Around him crew moved as if in a daze, or sat, weeping. As Tephe made his way forward, the air had begun to thin and grow cold. Behind him, he heard screaming and slow footfalls.

Tephe reached the command deck as the *Righteous* fell into darkness.

"Captain," Neal Forn said. "All of our systems are down. We have no power."

"I know," Tephe said, and pointed to the portal of the command deck. "Seal this portal," he said, to the crew on the command deck. "And once you seal it, block it. Place anything you can in front of it. Now." The crew moved at his command.

As the command deck portal shut, screams echoed down the walkways, close now.

Forn moved in close. "Captain, what is happening? We all *felt* something..."

"Our Lord is dead, Neal," Tephe said. "I saw Him die. All the gods He enslaved are free. They are leaving the ships."

"Without the gods, their crews will die," Forn said, whispering.

"Yes," Tephe said. "Sooner or later."

There were screams right outside the command deck now.

"And us, captain?" Forn said.

"We will die sooner," Tephe said, and turned to look at the command deck portal. There was what sounded like the clattering of knife points on it. "I am sorry, Neal. We will die much sooner."

The portal was hit by something mighty, and hit again. The portal caved and buckled as if it were made of pulled taffy.

"What should we do?" Forn asked his captain.

The portal was ripped from its hinges. Captain Ean Tephe turned to face his friend.

"Pray," he said.